# THE KEY PENDANT

## Louisa Rose

ISBN-13: 97988248164
ISBN-10: 97988248164

Cover design by: Art Painter
Library of Congress Control Number: 2018675309
Printed in the United States of America

*To my dad.  Gone but never forgotten.*

# CONTENTS

Title Page

Copyright

Dedication

Preface

The Key Pendant      1

Chapter 1      2

Chapter 2      8

Chapter 3      14

Chapter 4      18

Chapter 5      23

Chapter 6      29

Chapter 7      40

Chapter 8      47

Chapter 9      53

Chapter 10      61

Chapter 11      72

Chapter 12      78

Chapter 13      86

Chapter 14      92

Chapter 15      105

Chapter 16      110

Chapter 17     121

Chapter 18     124

Chapter 19     128

Chapter 18     140

Chapter 19     148

Chapter 20     157

Chapter 21     167

Day 1     170

Day 2     171

Day 28     172

Day 35     173

Day 49     174

Day 70     175

Day 100     176

Day 101     177

Day 63875     178

Chapter 22     179

Chapter 23     184

Chapter 24     190

Chapter 25     196

About The Author     199

# PREFACE

I started writing this book after having a recurring dream about a girl stuck in a room she had to find her way out of but never did.  As soon as I began scribbling in a notebook about twelve year old Alexandra and her adventures, the dreams stopped and, so far, have never resurfaced.

pepper
love always
Louisa
x

# THE KEY PENDANT

**Louisa Rose**

# CHAPTER 1

My name is Alexandra Heeton and I am finally happy. After almost a year of being bullied at school, my mom told the head teacher that I wouldn't be going back to that horrible place, and she would be home educating me instead. I don't think she made this decision lightly as in the last few months we had talked about me leaving school a lot and she knew how unhappy I was having to try to concentrate and learn in a place where I constantly felt under threat of verbal abuse and mind games with girls that pretended to be my friends. Since leaving the place I hated most in the world, my days have been filled with playing with my adorable little sister Beth, looking after our huge lion head rabbit called Sugarbomb (named after a sweet that tastes exactly like candyfloss and has a popping candy centre) and visiting a variety of different places like museums, castles and the library.

It's only been a few weeks since my awful experience at school ended, and a different kind of education began so we are doing something which is known to the home educating community as de-schooling. As I understand it this is a period (approximately one month for every year spent at school) in which you don't really do any kind of formal academic work (unless you want to of course) and mainly have fun playing and generally just being a kid. Mom says that in any case we are all learning all the time in everyday life, we never stop, and you don't need to sit at a desk looking at a workbook all the time to get a good education. I'm sure we will do some of that kind of work at some point (like when I'm studying for my

G.C.S.E's) but I don't think there's any rush at the moment, I am only twelve.

Today is Monday and usually I would be rushing out of the door with mom and Beth to get to school but at this moment in time I am lying in bed thinking about the past and the present. I can't believe how different my life is now and how amazingly free I feel. I wonder if those girls have moved on to someone else now and I worry about that. Why do bullies even exist? Why do they bully people? I just don't understand. Mom says it's probably because they are jealous, that the person they are picking on is a nicer person than them or more intelligent than they are. Maybe that's true. Perhaps bullies are just not happy with their own lives, so they try to make others unhappy to make them feel better about themselves. I don't really know but I just wish bullying would become as extinct as the dinosaurs are. It makes you panic a lot and feel so sad and lonely, like life is kind of hopeless.

Just as I am about to get out of bed and start getting dressed, I hear a bang! I race downstairs to find that Beth has fallen off the settee and is lying on the floor crying her eyes out. I scoop her up to give her a big cuddle as mom comes rushing in from the garden. After a few more tears and plenty more cuddles from mom and I, Beth calms down a bit. I start tickling her and before long we are both giggling and the fall (caused by my little gymnast-in-the-making sister trying to do some sort of new acrobatic move) appears to be ancient history. Checking that Beth is alright now and not really hurt, mom walks off into the kitchen saying she's going to make pancakes for breakfast. We are planning a trip to the park after we've eaten then maybe the library and a bit of food shopping to get something nice for tea.

Just then I hear mom say in a rather panicked voice "oh no, we've only got a tiny bit of milk left". I speed into the kitchen and tell her that I'll go to the shop and get some more. The shop is only at the end of our road in our quiet little village after all. I don't know how mom is going to react as I've never been anywhere on my own before but long to have a little bit of independence. After a few minutes of mom pacing backwards and forwards with one hand her hip and the other on her chin she finally says "ok but don't be long. Just go to the shop and then come straight back". Mom stares at me for a moment with a very serious look on her face. I know she worries but I am so glad she's letting me do this, it means such a lot.

Shutting the front door, I feel so grown up! At last, I have been allowed to do something by myself. I have looked forward to this moment for a long time. I breathe in the fresh summer air, noticing what a lovely warm sunny day it is. Birds are singing their sweet little tunes, a lady in a pretty pink dress pushing a sleeping baby in a pram passes me by and there's a beautiful big ginger cat over the other side of the road bathing in the summer sunshine. All is right with the world.

It only takes about ten minutes and I arrive at one of my favourite places. I absolutely love this shop. It's so quaint and so tiny, at least from the outside. There are just about every kind of sweet and chocolate you can imagine here and I'm pretty sure I know where each and every one of them live on the immaculately clean shelves that are all around the larger-on-the-inside it seems corner shop. There is also everything you might need to cook a meal from scratch along with household items like washing up liquid and shampoo. I really don't know how it all fits in but somehow it just does. The shop's owner Mr Ramsbottom is behind the counter with his duster as usual (he's always cleaning the shop). I say "Hi" and he jumps then turns around saying "oh gosh, you scared me!" I didn't mean to surprise him. I don't think he's used to having many customers come into the shop at this time of day. "I'm sorry Mr R" I say feeling a little bad that I startled him, "oh it's you um, um..." "Alex" I jump in knowing he always forgets my name. Well, I guess he is quite old. I like Mr Ramsbottom, he's always cheerful and friendly, seeming to genuinely care about how his customers are and what they are going to be doing with their day. Mr Ramsbottom has crazy grey hair that sticks up on top of his head and a very bushy moustache. He always wears a different brightly coloured tie every time I see him and today it is pink with yellow ducks all over!

After grabbing some milk, a small bag of teacakes for me and some fizzy dummies for Beth I hand over a £5 note and wait for my change. Just then a girl, a bit older than me I guess, walks into the shop. She has long blonde hair, (a world away from my own mousey brown mop) that waves beautifully down past her shoulders. She doesn't appear to be wearing any make up and is casually dressed in a t-shirt and skinny jeans that make her legs look like they go on forever. I wish I wasn't so short and that I'd worn something else, something more stylish than knee length shorts and a baggy oversized top. The girl walks towards me, smiles and says "hi". I feel a bit embarrassed but say "hi" back. She tells me she can't find a particular sweet she loves, rock candy and almost instantly I tell her exactly where they will be. There are small jars filled with different sized pieces at the back of the shop on a high shelf. I don't know why the girl asked me where to find the sweets and not Mr Ramsbottom as he's the one who owns this place, but I don't mention it. The girl goes to the back of the shop, grabs her small jar of sweets and puts the right amount of money on the counter. Mr Ramsbottom finally hands me my change and miss gorgeous, and I leave the shop at the same time. As we walk down the road together, I learn that the blonde girl's name is Meg, and she is nearly fourteen (although she looks more like sixteen). Meg likes climbing trees and playing football but also loves experimenting with different hairstyles and putting makeup on in her bedroom (then taking it all off before her dad sees her as he doesn't like her wearing it and she is not even allowed out with lip gloss on). Not that she needs make up. Meg is naturally pretty with large bright blue eyes and a few freckles around her nose. Even though she wears t-shirt and jeans she looks effortlessly stylish, one of those cool girls that I am always envious of. I'm wishing even more now that I had made more of an effort with my choice of clothing. I am too short and dumpy to make the combo I have on look remotely fashionable; I just grabbed the first thing I saw in my wardrobe as I wasn't really expecting to see many people on my first trip out by myself, not at this time of day anyway. Meg tells me she is also being home educated but not because of bullying or anything like that, she has never been to school, her parents decided to educate her themselves from the very beginning. I ask her how she feels about that, and she says she has always been happy learning at her own pace at home as well as being educated by everything in the world around her and that you can't miss what you never had anyway. I guess that makes sense. I'm kind of jealous. I wish I'd never been to school. As I open up about my experiences at school, I can see how shocked Meg is and can tell she feels bad for me and she is really listening, this just makes her more endearing and even cooler in my mind.

After walking and talking for the time it takes to arrive at the front gate of my house, we decide to swap phone numbers and Meg promises she will text me soon. We say goodbye giving each other a hug then Meg continues down the road, and I open the gate and make my way up the garden path feeling a little sad that I didn't get to spend more time chatting with the coolest, not to mention nicest friend I have ever made. I guess we will speak soon though and then we can arrange to meet up. As I approach the door it seems to open as if by magic. Mom has been watching out of the living room window eagerly waiting for me to come home and she looks extremely relieved to see that I am back alive and well. I know she worries but I figure that I can take care of myself if I really need to. I am stronger as a person now and not the same frightened little girl as I was not so long ago at school. As soon as I step foot into the hallway, I start talking about my interesting first independent journey and about my lovely new friend. Mom listens intently and seems genuinely interested. She's such a great mom and a good friend.

# CHAPTER 2

Since I met Meg two days ago, I have sent her some texts but not had one reply. Maybe she was a bit late back on the day we met and got into trouble with her dad (it seems like he's strict from what Meg told me about him) or maybe she was just being kind, humouring me by giving me her number and wasn't really interested in a younger, quite plain and pretty un-cool kid like me.

Another couple of days have gone by and I still haven't heard anything from Meg. Feeling like giving up on her I put my phone into my bag ready to take out with me on a trip to the museum. Then I hear my phone beep. I quickly retrieve it back out of my little black and white spotty bag and see I have a text from Meg! She's asking if I can meet her later today. I'm so happy right now, I run down the stairs excitedly to ask mom if I can meet up with Meg at the park (which is literally across the road from our house) when we come back from the museum. Mom thinks about it for a few minutes then says that I can go but that I mustn't be out for too long and am back to see dad before bedtime. Dad doesn't usually get back from work until after six, he works in a bank in the city, and it takes him a while to get home.

I'm so happy with my newfound freedom. I can't wait until 4.30 this afternoon at the park. Meg texted again after I replied to her previous text saying that I could meet up with her and told me she'd be waiting on the swings so I'd know where she would be. The park is huge with lots of different play areas and a duck pond in the middle that is more the size of a lake. I absolutely adore the museum with all the history it holds inside but secretly I want the trip to be over as quickly as possible so I can spend more time with the only friend I have that is remotely near my age. I wish I could fast forward time.

On the way to the museum, I look out of the window in the back of the car daydreaming about chatting about anything and everything and just messing about with my new friend. Beth is also looking out of the window, she looks so pretty with her purple butterfly top and pink leggings, silver T-bar shoes and an oversized bow in her golden blonde hair that ringlets so perfectly down her back. I love this little girl so much and we are so close, especially now that we get to spend so much time together. At almost five she is so much fun to play with. We bake cakes and biscuits together, play on the trampoline, talk about silly stuff which grown-ups wouldn't understand and so much more.

When we pull up at the museum, I undo my seatbelt then help Beth with hers before pulling the catch on the front seat and pushing it forward so I can get out of our funny little car via the front passenger door. Beth climbs out after me and we make our way with mom across the almost empty car park towards the front entrance to the huge museum. I really like this place with dinosaurs and early man right up to the 1960's to discover and learn about. History is my favourite subject, it's just so interesting learning about everything that has happened in the past, the world has changed so much, and I wonder what people in the future will think of the way we live right now. After having a good look around for a couple of hours and me trying to entertain a bored and hungry Beth we all decide it's best to head to the museum's cafe, I am starving, and I really need a drink. Beth and I share a glass of orange juice and a big wedge of homemade chocolate fudge cake which is so mouth-wateringly delicious that I am sure if heaven is a place, then this is what they must serve every day. Mom opts for a cheese sandwich and a cup of coffee which she seems to be enjoying although I think she secretly wishes she'd gone for the cake too. When we've all finished enjoying our refreshments, we decide to have a last look at the dinosaurs (Beth's favourite bit) before leaving this fantastic place and climbing back into our old Citroen 2cv and making our way home.

It has gone 4 o'clock when we pull up outside our house. I tell mom I'm going to get changed then go straight over to the park to meet Meg. I do not want to be late. As soon as I get inside, I run up the stairs and into my bedroom pulling my top off and flinging it onto the bed. What do I wear to meet up with someone as cool as Meg? I have no idea so open my wardrobe, close my eyes and swipe my hand slowly across all my clothes counting to five and saying "stop" out loud. I open my eyes and look at what I've picked. Ok not bad, could have been worse I suppose, I could have chosen my old school uniform, I'm not even entirely sure why I've still got it. I take off my shorts and step into my bright yellow playsuit, zipping it up at the side and tying the matching belt around my waist. Slipping my black high tops on, doing them up and grabbing my spotty bag I'm ready to go out.

On my short journey across the road and through the park to the swings I feel excited but a little nervous at the thought of meeting my glamourous new acquaintance. I hope Meg will become a real friend and nothing like those other girls from school. It's a little hard to trust people after what happened. I see her sitting on one of the swings. She looks stunning in a coral-coloured maxi dress, cropped denim jacket and black high tops just like mine! I find confidence in the knowledge that we have the same taste in footwear and with a better sense of self in this moment I find myself walking straight up to Meg saying "hi" quite confidently. We giggle about the fact that we have the same shoes on, and Meg tells me that it's a good job she didn't wear the yellow maxi dress she got last week because that would have been really weird. We talk about everything from fashion and makeup to which celebrity crushes we have. Meg finds it hilarious when I tell her who mine is, ok he's not everyone's idea of boyfriend material but I think he's cute in a curly haired cheeky face kind of way. As Meg's older than me, the boys she likes are older and not baby-faced boys that you could bring home to meet your mom with no worry of her showing them the door as soon as they've stepped foot through it.

The tone of the conversation changes and becomes more serious when Meg tells me I'm lucky to have a mom. "I'm sorry" I say, really meaning it and feeling empathy for her as I see tears welling in her beautiful cat-like blue eyes that are heavily filled with a deep sadness. She tells me her mom died three years ago and since then it's just been her and her dad. He is strict but Meg say's it's because he worries about her. The punishments he dishes out when he needs to seem harsh but it's only because he cares and is trying his best to teach her right from wrong. It's obvious to me that these words aren't really coming from Meg. I'm so glad my parents are different from a lot of others. They are more kind and understanding than Meg's dad sounds although I guess it must be tough being a single parent, my mom and dad have each other after all. I think for a moment about my family and the great relationship we all have, I am so lucky, I know I am. I feel even more lucky and sad at the same time for Meg when she tells me that her mom died from bowel cancer at just forty years old. My mom is nearly fifty and in pretty near perfect health as is my dad, well apart from the times when he has to have a lie down but maybe that's what you need to do when you are as old as my dad.

It's only been about forty minutes since I arrived at the park. Meg says that unfortunately she hasn't got much time until she needs to leave. Her dad wants her back for tea and she cannot be late. I tell her that I have enough money for a bag of chips to share and that the chip shop is only a short walk away. Meg says she better not. That her dad will be angry if she doesn't eat her tea and that she's not usually allowed fried chips anyway. Ok, I must admit, I am feeling less and less envious of Meg and more and more happy with my life, no proper chips, life would not be worth living!

As Meg and I start walking in the direction of Meg's house we see a boy on the other side of the road. He looks across at us and smiles. I feel myself going red with embarrassment and try my best to hide it then, oh no, he starts crossing the road. He's heading straight towards us! He has dark wavy hair that comes almost down to his shoulders. He's tall and slim but not too skinny and what he's wearing looks so cool, ripped jeans and a plain, oversized bright white t-shirt. The boy walks over to us and says "hi". Meg and I say "hi" back in unison and giggle a bit because of this and out of awkwardness (more on my part of course). The boy tells us his name is Chase and he lives in the next village. They don't have a chip shop where he lives so he's walked down to our village to get himself some tea. Chase flashes us the most gorgeous smile. His teeth are so white, they shine and sparkle like the rarest pearls and his eyes are the brightest turquoise blue, like infinity pools of tropical warm water. I could get lost looking into them. We tell Chase our names and each swap phone numbers with him before remembering what Meg had said about having to be home at a certain time. I tell her that we really need to get a move on. We say goodbye to Chase and continue walking towards Meg's house at a faster pace than before. I can't resist looking back and just as I do Chase turns too and winks. I turn straight back, blushing yet again.

Meg's startled voice breaks my thoughts of Chase and those eyes "Oh no!" she says looking at her watch, "it's five thirty! My dad's going to kill me!" "Ok, try to keep calm, I'll tell him it's my fault you're late, that I kept you chatting for too long and we lost track of time". Meg doesn't look at all convinced by my plan to appease her dad. She accepts what

I've suggested though as it's really the only option to hopefully not get into too much trouble. When we arrive at Meg's house her dad is holding back the dark coloured curtain and peering suspiciously out of the downstairs bay window. He looks worried I think and I kind of feel bad for him. The man just wants to protect his daughter. I can understand that. Meg's dad opens the door and throws his arms around her then pushes her away from him and tells her to go to her room. I try to say that it was my fault Meg was late back but before I can say two words the door is slammed shut in my face. OK I know Meg's dad was concerned but there was no need to be rude!

All the way home I think about what sort of punishment my friend will have to endure to make up for being late. I hope it's not too severe. I hope Meg's ok. As I reach home, I wonder if I should tell mom about how Meg's dad treats her. Mom won't approve as she's not like that at all and I don't want her speaking to Meg's dad about it in case Meg gets into even more trouble, so I decide it's not a good idea to tell her and keep what I know and feel to myself.

Later that evening, as I am getting ready for bed, I send Meg a text asking if everything's ok. I wait and wait and finally get a text back from Meg just as I am falling asleep which says that she is grounded for a week. I am so relieved. It could have been a lot worse. I was imagining all kinds of terrible punishments. Maybe Meg's dad isn't that bad after all.

# CHAPTER 3

I wake up at 8 o'clock the next morning and check my phone. There's a text from Chase saying he wants to meet up later today. Oh wow! I can't believe it. This is just too exciting. What on earth am I going to wear? Somehow, I need to try and sort this crazy mop out on my head before I can even think of going anywhere, especially to see those eyes and that smile again. I snap out of my Chase shaped daydream as I remember that Meg can't come. I am sure Chase won't have only asked me and that he invited the two of us. I'm not sure if I should go even though I massively want to. I text Meg to tell her and she replies almost instantly saying that she'll risk coming as her dad will be out for a few hours later so he won't notice she's gone if she gets back home before he does.

I am going to have to partially lie to mom about later and tell her that I'm just meeting Meg and not that a boy, an older one at that will be there too. I don't usually lie, I've not normally got any reason to, but I think this is different. I don't think mom will let me go if she knows I am meeting up with basically a stranger, the male variety anyway.

It's now 3 o'clock in the afternoon, precisely one hour until the meet up. I am far too nervous. I've already bitten my nails way more than I usually do and I still can't decide on the best outfit to wear. Right, I'm just going to go casual. T-shirt and jeans will do. I don't want to look like I've made too much effort, we are only meeting at the park after all. After taming my wild hair as best I can, applying a slick of mascara and lip balm, pulling on my grey top with a small black key motif on the front and faded jeans, I grab my bag and set off.

Meg and Chase are already sitting on the bench in the park. I feel nervous as I walk up to the coolest girl I have ever met and the gorgeous boy with the dreamy eyes I have befriended. I shouldn't have worried too much though because as soon as they see me, they both try to make me feel comfortable, each giving me a hug to say hi (Chase's hug lasting slightly longer than Meg's and feeling completely different especially as I awkwardly pull away in embarrassment). Before long I get over my shyness, putting my crush on Chase aside as we're all getting along so well, it's like we've known each other our whole lives. This is so much fun, laughing and joking with my two new friends. I feel like we're kindred spirits, the three of us. We talk about everything from things that have happened in our childhoods to what we want to be in the future. Meg wants to work in fashion. Chase isn't sure what he wants to do yet and I just want to be happy, whatever career I choose and whatever relationships I choose to have. I'm getting there, more so now I've met these two fantastic people. We all decide that we're hungry so take a walk down to the chip shop to share a bag of chips. Just as I was thinking of leaving, Chase mentions a party that's starting soon and asks us to come along with him. I guess I could text mom and tell her I would be a bit later than I had said but what about Meg? She is meant to be grounded, if her dad finds out she's snuck out she'll be in worse trouble. "I'm coming" Meg says. "Are you sure?" I ask, concerned. "I don't care what my dad says or thinks, I'm sick of him treating me like a little kid, lead the way Chase" Meg says, meaning every word, I can tell.

After walking for about ten minutes, we come to a large, old, creepy looking house. It's like something from a horror film, grey walls and windows you can't see through. This is not what I was expecting at all. The house stands alone on the edge of a field with the road in front of it and a forest in the background. I get a strange feeling as I walk with my friends up the path towards a large dark wooden door. I feel like I sort of recognise this place, I don't know why or how but the feeling that I've been here before is making me feel a little uneasy. Chase knocks on the door and I hear a friendly male voice. "Go around to the back please" the boy says. As we make our way around to the back of this huge old house, I realise I can't hear any music playing which is quite strange as there is supposed to be a party going on, in fact I can't hear anything at all, it's perfectly silent. When we reach the back of the house, I see that the windows have been boarded up which makes me feel even worse, I am freaking out a bit and actually feel like running all the way back home, but I don't, I don't want to come across as a silly little girl who just wants her mommy so I just wait at the back door with the others.

Chase is just about to knock on the door when it opens. "Come on in" says a good-looking boy dressed like a waiter from a restaurant. As I step inside the house, I am more shocked than I think I've ever been about anything before. It's nothing like I expected it to be, nothing like how the outside looks. It doesn't match or make sense at all. It's white and modern and it's spotlessly clean. It appears to be brand new inside, but the outside tells a different story. I don't get it. "Drink anyone?" asks the boy who answered the door to us. "We have larger, cider, vodka, wine, you name it, we have something for everyone here. What would you all like?" he asks, then grins widely. Chase opts for lager; Meg cider and I go with a diet cola. "Coming right up" says the boy, this time with a stern look. I say boy but now as I look at him again it's obvious that he's not as young as I first thought, he's a man.

Meg and Chase seem to not have noticed how strange this house is and sit down on shiny white plastic chairs that have thin silver legs, sipping their drinks from tall, fragile looking glasses. They chat and giggle together, seeming to be without a care in the world. I guess Meg is making the most of her bit of freedom. I'm not sure about Chase. I wonder how he knew about this house and who could have invited him to this so-called party. He didn't seem to know the waiter so I wouldn't have thought it was him who sent an invitation. I try to tell Meg that I'm going to find the toilet but I'm not sure she even hears me. She's deep in conversation with Chase and already seems tipsy.

I haven't got a clue where the toilet is and don't really need it, but I am curious about this house so decide, maybe against my better judgement to explore a little before leaving. There aren't many people here and it's not my idea of what a party should be although it's not like I've got much experience of parties. I'm not sure family get-togethers really count. As I walk along a stark, glossy white hallway I notice a spiral staircase that looks as if it is made of glass. I've always loved climbing staircases, needing to know what was at the top and this delicate looking winding one is no different, I must know what it leads to.

As I reach the top of the staircase after only a few moments, I look down and to my horror can barely see the floor below. With my heart pounding and feeling that I might pass out at any moment I take the final step and realise I am now in a very small room. My head feels funny, the room spins, and everything turns black.

# CHAPTER 4

I open my eyes and look up. The roof is made of glass and as I look around, I realise I am in a much bigger room now than I was in when I'd reached the top of the spiral staircase. I manage to sit up slowly, my head feeling fuzzy and my body heavy. Where has the staircase gone? I climbed it so I know it was there before. This room seems too big to fit into the house but I am in the house so it must fit. There are no doors or windows here just glossy white walls, a shiny black floor and the glass roof. How am I going to get out? I get up from the floor that is so polished I can see my reflection in it and start to walk towards one of the walls. There is nothing on the wall. Not a mark, a cobweb, a speck of dust. I can't believe I'm inside the creepy looking dilapidated old house. It's so clean and new looking in here. I wonder how the roof can be made of glass when it didn't look like glass from outside. Feeling confused, scared and like I'm about to burst into tears, I turn to walk to the other side of the room and see something that I swear was not there before. There's a large box at the far end of the room. As I make my way towards the box it seems to get smaller and smaller the closer I get until, as I approach it, I can reach down, pick it up and hold it in my hand. I kneel on the cold hard floor and open the tiny golden box. There's a card inside that reads 'go to sleep'. How can I possibly fall asleep at this moment in time and why should I? Who put this box here and what is this all about? I don't know what to do.

After what seems like forever and not being able to think of anything else to do, I finally decide that my only option is to try and do what the card says and fall asleep. I look up and see a bed in the middle of the room. That was certainly not there before. I walk over to the huge wooden bed thinking how comfortable it looks. I get an overwhelming urge to climb into it and snuggle down. It's the only thing I want to do right now. Maybe I can hide under the covers until this weird evening ends and then I can go back home. I'm not sure I feel sleepy enough to be able to fall asleep but get into the bed and lie down anyway, willing to try. Perhaps I need to fall sleep inside this dream I am obviously in to be able to wake up again. Yes, that's it, this is all a dream. I feel so cosy and warm underneath what feels like a duck down quilt. Strangely, I don't feel scared and confused now, safer and content, like I'm being given a big hug from someone I trust. I close my eyes for a moment suddenly feeling sleepy. Somewhere between being awake and asleep I open my eyes to see that I am not in the bed anymore or in the room, not even in the house. I am standing on the edge of a cliff looking out at the most beautiful turquoise sea I have ever seen.

I feel emotional looking at the ocean but also calm, serine, like nothing else matters but this moment. I feel something in my hand. I look down and see that it is a small round mirror. I hold the mirror up and look at my reflection. The mirror shows me an older version of myself. I look maybe thirty-five or forty. What on earth is going on? This can't be real, any of it, I must be dreaming, that's the only answer I can think of that makes any sense. I want to scream, thinking maybe that will wake me up but when I open my mouth, nothing comes out. Not a sound. I feel a tap on my shoulder and turn around to see a woman with short blonde hair and blue eyes looking at me. It's Meg, I know it is, but she too looks much older. "What's going on Meg" I ask. She doesn't answer and instead turns around and starts walking. I catch up and try talking to her, but she doesn't respond and just continues walking. I look ahead and see what appears to be a very dense looking forest. The trees that make up the forest are very tall, and I feel nervous as we get further towards it but continue to follow Meg all the same without a thought of turning back. As we enter the forest I feel a chill, it's much colder than it was just, when we were out in the open. I look back now but can only see trees behind me. The ground crunches with every step I take, and I realise I am walking on freshly fallen pure white snow.

After a considerable amount of time, we come to a clearing. There in front of me stands a small white building the size of a dolls house. I wonder how I would fit inside (if I even wanted to that is) but the closer I get, the larger it seems to get until it's the size of an actual house humans could enter. The exterior is white and glossy, like the interior of the old house I fell asleep in and somehow managed to escape from. Meg pushes the door open, and I follow her inside, quite apprehensively. I'm shocked to find that just as the old house appeared new inside, this brand-new looking house appears to be very old inside. There are wooden beams on the ceiling of what I presume is the living room and a majestic looking fireplace with a wood burner that has been set ablaze. I can't feel my hands, they are so cold and numb now because of the freezing temperature outside and not having any gloves with me so I decide to go over to the inviting fire and warm up. After a few moments by the fire, I turn around to see that Meg is sitting on a dark brown leather settee which looks so familiar, it's just like our settee at home with a high back and deep cushions. The comfortable looking settee reminds me so much of home, oh how I wish I was there right now instead of here, wherever here is. Wiping away the tears that are welling in my eyes I start to look around. There are pictures everywhere of different objects, places and people. I see one with a cliff just like the one I stood at the edge of, overlooking the sea and another of a duck pond that looks equally familiar. Every picture I look at seems to be of somewhere I've been or someone I recognise, objects I've touched but most I can't quite remember, like they are all memories that have sort of been locked away somehow. I look behind me to see what Meg is doing but she's not there. Suddenly I feel the ground underneath me moving, like I'm on a boat. I go to the door and open it only to find that the house is in fact floating on water. I shut the door again quickly, walk across to the settee and sit down putting my head in my hands, utter confusion consuming me. This isn't real, this isn't real I chant over and over until a tiny meow seems to snap me out of my trance like state. I look down at my feet to see a small fluffy blue kitten looking up at me. It looks familiar, the same as the pictures did and this old settee, I feel like I already know this little cat and like it knows me.

The blue ball of fluff jumps onto my lap. I start stroking it and it, in turn, starts to purr. I must give it a name. I decide on Henry which was my granddads name. He was such a lovely man my granddad, always baking and making his own jam, the smells from his kitchen were amazing. I'd go round to granddads cottage in the next village from our own and sample all the good things he'd made. There were two apple trees in the back garden, one a large cooking apple tree and the other a smaller eating apple variety. In the winter we'd have warm apple pie or crumble that granddad had made from scratch. He was an amazing cook and I always looked forward to whatever delights were waiting for me when I went round to his house.

I loved being in the garden at granddads, I used to climb both apple trees, help in the garden watering the flowers, planting seeds and picking the vegetables that were in abundance in the large patch. Most of my favourite memories are of times spent at granddads, I smile while thinking of him then remember that I'll never see him again, he passed away last year. I couldn't face going to the funeral, it was all too upsetting, too overwhelming for me at the time. My granddad and I were just so close. I felt like I'd lost a parent. I'd give anything for granddad to walk in here right now and tell me that everything is going to be ok, that I've had a bad dream and now I've woken up and he's there for me but that's not going to happen, I know it. Henry looks up at me from my lap with his beautiful eyes, one orange, one green and I swear he winks at me. I rub my eyes in disbelief and look at him again. He just stares at me for what seems like ages than suddenly jumps down from my lap and runs off.

"Henry, come back!" I run after him out of the living room and into a long hallway. Henry is not there but I see a bright blue door at the end of the hallway that I start walking towards then find that I am already there. I reach for the silver doorknob but as I do the door automatically opens. I gasp at what I see before me, a huge transparent underwater tunnel. As I step inside the tunnel onto a see-through floor I see brightly coloured tropical fish, sharks, stingrays and coral all around me. I feel uneasy being able to see straight through the floor below even though the view is amazing but keep putting one foot in front of the other until the tunnel ends. When I get to the end of this miraculous tunnel, I notice that there isn't a door, just a cave wall. I look back to find that the other end of the tunnel is the same and that there is no door at the beginning of the tunnel either. So how did I get in? I start to panic, shouting "help, help" and banging on the sides of the tunnel but it's no use, there is no one out there and even if there were I doubt they would hear me anyway. There's no way out, I'm trapped. I sit down and look at the fish below me. They seem to be looking at me, trying to work me out, all of them at the same time each in unison with the next. I stare at them as they stare back at me then I hear a meow and the fish swim away. I look up to find that I am not in the tunnel under the sea anymore.

# CHAPTER 5

I am back in the perfectly clean, white living room of the old house. There is nobody here but myself, Henry and a small boy of about four or five years of age standing in front of me. "Hello" I say to the little boy who has a worried expression on his face. "What's your name?" I ask. "I can't remember" replies the boy. "Well, my name is Alex" I say looking into his sparkly bright blue eyes and notice his hair is wavy and dark brown in colour. It's uncanny, this little boy looks like a smaller, younger version of Chase. There is something different about him though, I can't describe it, but I feel like I want to protect him. The boy doesn't know how he got here, he can't remember, but he feels scared and just wants to go home. I tell him I want to go home too and that I also miss my parents to which he looks puzzled. I then remember that although I am only twelve, I look like an adult now. I try to assure the boy that I am just a kid inside but he just giggles and clearly doesn't understand so I leave it at that. "Right, let's get out of here and find our way home" I say, not feeling very confident but trying to show that I mean every word I say.

I open the front door into a vast green field that seems to go on forever. As I peer into the distance, I see something moving towards us but can't make out yet what it is. Henry, the boy and I step out into the field and the door closes behind us. As I turn back, expecting to see an uninviting monstrosity of a building which I'm glad to be outside of I see that the house seems to have disappeared. There is nothing but grass underfoot and clear blue sky above, well apart from whatever it is that is coming towards us. As the thing gets closer, I see that it's a person, a girl, it's Meg. "Come on, quickly, follow me" Meg tells us, hurrying us along. I scoop Henry up with one hand and hold the boy's hand with the other, walking quickly. As we rush on through the field as fast as we possibly can Meg looks back at the boy then at me with a confused look on her face. She says nothing and continues to lead us onto goodness only knows where.

After a while we come across a small grey stone well. It's so pretty, like something from a picture on a postcard of a chocolate box village, our village, this is the same as the wishing well near our park, I'm sure of it. "Start climbing" Meg says looking at me. "What?" I ask. "What do you mean?" "Start climbing down inside the wishing well" replies Meg with an unnerving urgency in her voice and a serious look on her face. With nothing else in sight anywhere around us as well as feeling a need to get away from whatever is spooking Meg, I decide we that must climb down and see where the ladder inside the wishing well takes us. I put Henry down on the grass and pull myself up onto the edge of the wishing well then put one foot down onto the first rung of the dark metal ladder. The boy picks Henry up and hands him back to me. I'm going to have to carry him. As I start climbing down rung by rung with the others following, the inside of the well lights up. There are fireflies in here, all around us, hundreds of them lighting our way. They give off a beautiful glow and if I wasn't making my way down a well, not knowing what is at the bottom, looking like an adult but feeling very much like a child I would think it was lovely.

The climb down seems to go on forever and isn't that easy to do when you're only using one hand to hold onto the ladder because you have a small shivering kitten in the other. When I finally reach the bottom, I step onto what feels like thick carpet. It's quite dark down here as the fireflies are above us, staying higher up in the well. There is a small amount of light coming into the room we are now in that's coming from behind a door in front of us. Meg opens the door which, to my amazement and shear horror reveals the white room with the glass roof where all this started. "NO!" I shout at the top of my voice. "Shhh, they might hear you" Meg says pressing her finger tightly to her lips, shaking her head and frowning. "Who's 'they'?" I ask but Meg doesn't answer and just walks off into the white room closing the door behind her. I turn the handle on the door, but it is now locked. I try again and again but it's no use, it won't budge. The boy starts to cry so I give him a cuddle and tell him it's ok and that everything will be fine but inside I know it's far from that. It's dark in here now. The light from behind the door has gone out and the fireflies that were above have disappeared. I crouch down and feel the soft carpet, familiarity hitting me again. Crawling around on my hands and knees I discover what feels like a candle. I don't have any matches so I can't light it. It's no use at all. I drop the candle back down on the floor and lie down feeling utterly exhausted.

I wake to find Henry licking my face and the boy calling my name. "Alex, Alex, I found something!" He puts what feels like a small box in my hand. I slide the box open and find a match inside. I scrabble around on the floor for the candle I dropped earlier until I find it and sit down, placing it between my knees then strike the match and light the candle. I am not in a room at the bottom of a well anymore. I am in my bedroom, and I am alone.

I don't know how I am back here or where Henry and the boy are, but they are not with me. I hope they've found some other way out and are not still trapped in that room. Looking around my bedroom everything appears to be exactly as I left it. My hairbrush and body spray are on the dressing table in front of the mirror and my teddy bear that I've had since the day I was born is sitting upright on my pillow. Nothing is out of place but still something doesn't feel right in here. I walk over to the window and look outside. Everything looks the same as usual. The post box still stands on the pavement over the other side of the road, and I can see the park beyond it. Still, I can't shake the feeling that something's not right then, as I turn around, I see the photo stuck to the mirror. There's nothing unusual about the photo being there, I stuck it on the mirror a few weeks ago with. It is what is on the photo that is strange. It should be a photo of mom, dad, Beth and I standing outside the castle we had visited a while back but instead I am standing there with Meg, Henry and the boy. In the photo I am wearing the same clothes I have on right now and everyone looks the same as they did before they vanished earlier. I turn around and head for my bedroom door. I need answers and hopefully mom can help if she's here. I open the door and stop as if instantly rooted to the spot. Here before me is the castle in the photo. I swallow hard, take a deep breath and step forward towards it.

When I get to the castle's drawbridge, I hear my name being called and turn around. Meg and the boy are standing right beside me, and Henry is now in my arms. I wonder how I saw the photo of us here before it was even taken. "Meg please, I can't take much more of this, tell me what's going on!" I beg my friend. Meg doesn't answer but instead I hear a voice coming from behind us. "It's easier if I just show you Alex". I turn around and see an old lady with grey hair and thick framed glasses. "Follow me" the lady commands, then begins walking away from the castle. After looking at one another for some reassurance Meg shrugs her shoulders and I nod my head, somehow feeling like this should be happening, like it's right. I start walking after the mysterious elderly lady across the field with Henry in one arm and the boy holding my free hand.

The lady stops at a gate with beautiful pink and white flowers all around it. There's nothing either side of the gate. There are no walls or even a fence, just the gate standing here in the middle of the field. I remember this gate, it's the one from granddads garden, I am sure of it. What's the point of going through a gate when there's nothing beyond it? All I can see through the cast iron bars is grass. As the gate opens, I gasp. What I see is mesmerising, my idea of what heaven should look like. I wonder for a moment if I have died, and this is in fact the gate to divine eternity. Maybe God does exist.

As I make my way through the open gate, I feel warmth on my skin. It suddenly turns humid, like how it would feel to be in a tropical rain forest I imagine. I look up and see a brightly coloured bird in a tree and ahead on the side of the pathway is a tiger, an actual real live tiger sleeping (I hope). "Don't worry" says the old lady, "it won't wake up". Still, I hold my breath as I walk past the huge, majestic and very dangerous looking animal.

We come across a little bridge over a babbling stream which makes me feel the same as I did when I stood on the edge of the cliff overlooking the sea, shear contentment. As I walk over the bridge, I let the feeling wash over me until, as I step off the other side, it's gone, and I am back to feeling a mixture of confusion, fear and curiosity all in equal measure.

After walking a little further, I see a table in the middle of the path. It's elaborately decorated with silver candlesticks, pink and white flowers in gold vases and every sweet treat imaginable. In the centre there is a tall glass jug just like the one mom brings out on special occasions. It's filled with what looks like real lemonade. Henry suddenly jumps out of my arms and leaps up onto one of the chairs that have been placed all around the table which is odd because he couldn't have done that not too long ago as he was too little, he appears to have grown bigger in the last few seconds. There are six chairs altogether, one for me, one for Meg, one for the boy, one for Henry, one for the old lady and one extra one. After we have all made ourselves comfortable on deep purple crushed velvet chairs that strangely pull themselves out for each of us, the old lady asks us to wait for the last guest to arrive before we start delving into the delights before us. I can almost taste the fresh and juicy looking strawberries and the sweet and sour lemonade when I hear footsteps behind me.

# CHAPTER 6

I turn around to see a young man wearing a bright red bow tie with what looks like pictures of yellow sweets on it. He has white-blonde hair that sticks out in all directions reminding me of the friendly old man who owns the corner shop back in my little village. It can't be him though, this man is much younger, a bit taller and anyway if it was really him how did he get here? I tell myself that this man isn't Mr Ramsbottom then he starts to speak. It is him, a different version of him but him all the same. Young Mr Ramsbottom looks at Henry and says hello. Henry meows as if he understands him, more than that, he appears to know him. As bizarre as this all is, I feel comfortable which could be something to do with this chair being so soft and luxurious but mainly because of the atmosphere around this table which is warm and reassuring. I clear my throat, and everyone stops to looks at me. "Um, can someone please tell me where I am?" Young Mr Ramsbottom smiles and says, "don't worry, you're perfectly safe here". I smile back non-the wiser and still wondering where 'here' is but don't ask again. I don't think I'm going to get the answers to the questions swirling around in my head now.

I'm not sure why but I feel I want to look up. The sky is a perfect shade of cornflower blue and there isn't a cloud in it. As I look up at the sky for a few moments longer wondering why my eyes aren't watering yet as it is clearly a very sunny day, I see something that I hadn't noticed before. It's a sort of shimmer, like there's thin layer high up in the sky. I look back at the table, there's nothing on it now, I haven't eaten anything yet and I'm starving. "Where has all the food gone?" I ask feeling like I am going to cry. Young Mr Ramsbottom reaches for his now much bigger bow tie and seems to take something from it. He slides it across the table to me and I pick it up. It's a wrapped sweet. The more eccentric than I usually know him to be man plucked an actual sweet from his tie! I pull the twisted ends of the bright yellow wrapping and the sweet falls onto the table in front of me. It's small, shiny and red in colour and as I pick it up and hold it in my hand it starts growing until it's the size and shape of a large strawberry. I am so hungry and the huge sweet looks so appetizing that I can't help but take a bite. The gorgeous taste of perfectly ripe strawberry hits me then zingy lemonade with a hint of fresh mint. I take bite after bite until I have finished the whole thing then everything starts going fuzzy and blurred and I start drifting into a deep sleep.

I wake up and slowly stretch my whole body out, yawning and opening my eyes. I am in my room again, in my bed with my lovely thick cosy quilt and super soft pillows that my head sinks into. I was here earlier, and it wasn't real, so I don't hold out much hope that this is real now. I get up, go over to the mirror and look at my reflection in it. Yes! I am my twelve-year-old self again, that's a relief. I cast my eyes to the family photo with the castle, this time looking how it should with mom, dad, Beth and I standing there together, me wearing the clothes I was wearing on the day the photo was taken. I turn around and move over to the window looking out to see heavy rain which makes a change from all the sun, blue sky and heat I have been experiencing lately. I walk over to my bedroom door, take a very deep breath then exhale slowly and quickly open the door. There's the landing and the staircase, it all looks normal thankfully so maybe I am back home, maybe it was all just a very vivid and strange dream.

I run downstairs to find Beth dressed as a superhero, playing with her soft toys and rush over to give her the biggest cuddle ever. She smells so good, all fruity shampoo and chocolate rolled into one. Beth always makes me feel better, even on my most down days. After that crazy journey or dream, whatever it was I'm just glad to be back with my amazing little sister. "I love you so much" I say, looking into Beth's eyes and she tells me she loves me back throwing her arms around my neck and giggling. "Mom" "Dad!" I let go of Beth and run over to them hugging them both as hard as I possibly can. "I've missed you both so much" I say, grateful that they are here with me now. "It's only been about eight hours silly sausage" says dad and I realise it must be morning, I've slept all night. "So, you saw me last night?" I ask my dad, now with a puzzled look on his face. "Of course, Alex, I tucked you in as I usually do, and you drifted right off, out like a light you were." I'm so confused, I'm sure I didn't even make it home last night let alone go to sleep in my own bed.

"Come on, come and have some breakfast before you get ready for school" says mom. "What do you mean school?" I ask, now even more confused. "Alex, it's Monday morning, come on you don't want to be late; you've got art this morning, your favourite lesson". Maybe leaving school and being home educated was a dream too, the last few months hadn't really happened, I didn't go to the corner shop that day and meet Meg and we never met Chase but how could they have been in my dream if I've never met them? It was all so real, it can't have been a dream, it just can't. "Mom, Meg wants me to go and meet her later" I say. Mom has a blank expression on her face. "Whose Meg?" she asks. "Um, a new girl from school" I say thinking that it's better to lie about who Meg is than sound like a crazy person going on about someone who is or isn't real. "I don't think so Alex" says mom explaining that we're going round to granddads for tea after school. "What, granddads alive?" I ask stunned. "What on earth is the matter with you this morning Alex?" Dad asks me, looking concerned. I tell him I just had a weird dream that I was in the future or an alternate reality where everything was different but similar and my granddad was dead. I tell mom and dad not to worry about me and that it was just a stupid dream as I sit down at the small drop leaf kitchen table. I grab a slice of white toast from a stack piled high on a plate, spread it with butter from the glass butter dish and spoon out some strawberry jam from a jar beside it. It's granddads homemade jam. I love the way it tastes, it's amazing, just the right amount of sugar to fruit, not too sweet and a little sour. I am so glad that my wonderful granddad is alive and smile when as I think about him then something changes in my brain like someone has just flicked a switch and my thoughts turn to school and a feeling of dread starts to sink in like water dripping onto metal making it rust and tarnishing all my good thoughts.

I worry all the way on the long walk to school. As I arrive at the gates, I look ahead to the place I have not missed seeing one bit. It looks the same as it did the last time I saw it, which to me seems like months ago but apparently was only last Friday. I can't even remember what I did on the weekend in fact I can't remember anything that's supposed to have happened and all I keep thinking about is the dream. I would rather be anywhere else right now than here outside school. The dread I feel is almost all consuming and it takes all I have in me just to pass through the gates and step onto the playground. I wish I was asleep, back in my dream in the tropical paradise where everything was unusual but somehow felt comforting and right.

Gulping hard, I step towards the door. That's odd, there's no one here, no children, no teachers. It's too quiet. I open the heavy metal framed glass door and step inside the still and silent school building. There's the long corridor with all the classrooms down each side opposite each other the same as it always was. There is student's artwork on the walls and that oh so familiar smell of disinfectant as the floors are always cleaned early in the morning before anyone gets here. At the other end of the corridor, I see a ladder. I walk towards it glancing from side to side as I pass each classroom which all appear to be empty. Where is everyone? I don't understand. Maybe I'm just early and no one's arrived yet. But if that is the case then surely the cleaner would be here at least. Who unlocked the gates and the door? There must be someone here. "Hello" I say loudly but my voice just echoes around the empty corridor, and no one answers.

I have now reached the ladder which, as I look up, seems to go on forever as I can't see the top. I must climb it; I can't help myself. I need to know what's up there. As soon as I step on the first rung of the ladder I am already at the top. Ok, well that's not strange at all. I climb out of the well that I'd gone down yesterday or today or in twenty years from now, I have no idea of time let alone where I am or what is happening to me. One thing's for sure, I am not in school anymore.

I'm standing in a field. The sky is blue, the air warm and I am alone. Hang on, what's that sound? I hear something in the distance and start walking towards it. As I get closer, I hear the sound more clearly, it's a very faint meow. It's Henry, it's got to be. I see the forest in front of me from the last time I was here and walk towards it and closer to the meow. When I get there, I step off the grass then between two tall trees and into the forest feeling that same familiar chill that I felt before. I see a large blue cat in front of me. It's Henry, I'm sure of it, just bigger, older. I run up to him and he jumps into my arms. He feels so soft, his fur is thick, and I sink my fingers into it as I cuddle him. "Oh Henry, it's so good to see you, you've got so big!" I say looking lovingly at the majestic creature feeling happy that he's here with me but worried about where the boy could be. Henry stares at me with those beautiful orange and green eyes and looks almost like he's smiling.

I look up and see the shimmer above in the clear blue sky. I am determined to find out what this is all about and start walking with Henry by my side. I decide I am going to find where the shimmer ends and discover what is beyond it. I see the white building but this time I am not tempted to go inside and instead walk past it and carry on towards the other end of the forest. Parting the low branches of the last few trees I am pleased to feel warmth again as I am so cold, I feel chilled to my core. There's the castle right in front of us, the one I saw here before and the same one that's in my photo. As I start walking past the castle it appears to wobble. I touch the wall and sure enough it feels like jelly and seems to be melting away before my very eyes into the ground until it is gone. Henry and I continue our mission to find the end of the shimmer, leaving just a grey puddle behind where the castle used to be.

I see it in the distance, the shimmer, and quicken my pace with Henry doing the same to keep up with me. As we get closer the shimmer gets brighter and I feel heat coming from it. Even though it's transparent it looks like a thin wall. I reach out to touch it but it's too hot, like the inside of an oven. I look down for Henry but he's not there. I look back up and there he is on the other side of the transparent wall, but he's a kitten again. I wonder how he made it through without getting burnt and how he'd suddenly got younger like time had rewound just for him. I put my hands close to the wall being careful not to touch it and move slowly trying to find a cooler part I can touch or a clue as to how to get through but there's nothing, it's all the same. Frustrated and close to tears I slump down on the ground.

I feel a tickle on my hand and look down at it to discover a ladybird sitting there looking up at me. The tiny creature has four black spots on a bright yellow body which makes it the most unusual ladybird I've ever seen having only ever seen the black and red one's before. We stare at each other, the insect and I until it flies off making me jump with surprise. I look around for the black and yellow ladybird then it flies right up to my face and hovers there for a few moments. I feel like it wants me to follow it, like it's guiding me somewhere, so I get up and start walking in the direction it flies. I can't believe I missed this, there's a gap in the wall but I can only see it now because the ladybird is showing me how to. It hovers close to the wall and then flies slowly to the right then out the other side. I get close to the wall the same way the ladybird did, in the same place and look down the wall to my right, there it is, there's the gap. I carefully take side steps until I am through and on the other side.

Nothing looks like it did when I was on the inside. When I was the other side of the shimmer, I saw green grass and blue sky now all I see is grey. I'm standing on a street with no colour anywhere. The houses all look the same, all grey, all drab, this place is depressing. I watch the ladybird fly back through the gap and I've got to admit I am tempted to follow it but don't. Instead, I step onto the pavement and start walking. I can't see Henry, he was here before I went through the gap but now, he's not, it's like he's vanished. I walk past grey houses with grey doors and grey walls feeling like I am in some old black and white movie. I can't believe my eyes when I see a thin bright red house ahead sandwiched between two large grey ones. The red house has a royal blue coloured door that I really must knock on, I can't walk past it. There's no answer so I try the doorknob to see if it turns. I guess I should know better by now than to let my curiosity get the better of me. Maybe I should have carried on down the road searching for Henry instead of trying to get inside this quirky little house, but I can't help myself, I must know what's inside.

The door opens as I turn the knob and I see two more doors directly in front of me. One door is large and white with burgundy velvet curtains either side of it and the other is smaller, wooden and looks quite old. I turn around, the red door is still there and still open, so I now have three options, try to open the white door, try to open the wooden door or go back out of the house. I could go back and continue to look for Henry but what if I don't find him and instead just endlessly walk up and down grey streets feeling more and more desperate and hopeless by the second? What if I do find him, what then? Anyway, Henry could have come into this house. He could be the other side of one of these doors. I decide there's no point in going back so now I need to choose a door and then try to open it.

For some reason I have an overwhelming feeling to look up just like when I first saw the shimmer over the sky and see something shining up by the ceiling. It's an extremely high ceiling, I can barely see it but there's something up there. I look at the wall to the left of me and notice some notches sticking out that I'm sure weren't there before, they look like they form some sort of a pattern. Maybe I could climb the wall. I'm good at climbing after hauling myself up the apple tree's so often in granddads garden. Maybe the shiny thing is a key that will open one of the doors. Neither door has a keyhole, so it won't be much use if it is a key, but I still must get up there and find out what it is.

Here goes. I put my foot on a lower notch and my hand on a much higher one and start the climb. After a few minutes I am about halfway up I think and make the mistake of looking down. The floor looks such a long way away now, I can hardly see it but still I look back up and continue the climb towards the shiny thing. As I get closer, I see that it is a small mirror. Is that all it is? What use is a mirror to me at this moment in time? I take the mirror, all the same, put it in my pocket and start making my way back down the wall.

Travelling down seems a much shorter journey than on the way up and I am back down on solid ground before I know it. I still have the decision of which door to choose and now I am shattered after my climb to collect a small mirror that is seemingly of no use at all. Standing here thinking about what I should do but not coming up with any answers, I realise I haven't even looked in the mirror yet. Maybe I can get some sort of clue from it. Maybe I'll see what I should do. I'm not at all sure that I want to look into the mirror as the last time I saw my reflection in a handheld one, I was a different me. I hold the small mirror up to peek all the same, feeling ever so slightly braver. I am relieved to see that I am me, the normal child version. I breathe a sigh of relief then see something else in the mirror, something behind me. Mom, dad and Beth are there in the mirror. I look around but they're not standing behind me in this hallway. I look back into the mirror and they are again just as a reflection. They look like they are all saying something at the same time but there's no sound. I look closer desperately trying to lip read then I realise what they're saying, they're calling my name.

I shout out "mom, dad" but it's no use, they can't hear me. I am here and they are there, we are in two separate places. It looks bright and clean, the room my family are standing in. I look back at the two doors that are so different from one another, trying to decide what to do. The white door reminds me of that large room with the glass roof in the creepy house. The wooden door resembles the back door at granddads, well the door to the veranda that you had to go through to get to the actual back door to the house. This should be an easy decision really thinking of how much the wooden door reminds me of days gone by stepping inside the veranda and feeling instant warmth (due to the fact it was mostly made of glass) then opening the back door that led to the kitchen one way and the toilet the other. I don't know why (maybe because there is a small possibility in a corner of my mind that my family will be behind it) but I am more drawn to the other door, the white one.

I lie face down on the floor and try to look underneath the wooden door for clues as to what is behind it. There is a small gap and I see a glow from what a think is a fire. There are feet from what I presume belong to a chair also. I hear what sounds like sniffing right behind the door then a meow. It's Henry! I'd know the sound he makes anywhere, different from any other cat I've ever met, like he's really trying to communicate with me. This should make my mind up even more about which door to choose but still I can't shake the feeling that I should find out what's behind the white one.

I lift the mirror to take another look at the reflection. Mom, dad and Beth are still there, silent but I know they are calling my name. I hear Henry meow and long to pick him up and cuddle him but still the desire to open the white door is there deep within me and getting stronger by the second. There's no gap underneath the white door and no sound when I put my ear to it, so I have no clue what's behind it whatsoever yet still I push it and it opens.

The light is blinding. When I can open my eyes and focus again, I see my mom standing over me. I realise that I am lying down on a bed with my family and Meg around me. "Oh Alex, you're awake" says mom. "What's going on?" I manage feeling exhausted. "Meg, you're here, you're real!" I say, surprised but relieved to see her. "Ha, of course I'm real silly" Meg replies with a slightly uneasy tone to her voice. Mom starts to explain that after coming back from meeting Meg a few months ago I had seemed troubled and started talking about things that didn't make sense, acting like I didn't trust anyone and didn't seem to know what reality was. I was completely paranoid apparently. I went to the doctors after still being the same a week later and he gave me a prescription for tablets to help with the way I was feeling and calm me down. Mom said she wasn't entirely comfortable with the thought of me taking medication, but the doctor had assured her it was for the best.

So, I've been on drugs. That's why my head feels fuzzy. Maybe the whole experience of the last few days had only been in my mind, or I had woken up from a very long and bizarre dream. Dad tells me that after around a month of being on the tablets I wasn't getting any better, so I went to stay in a hospital for a while. Apparently, I've had a complete mental breakdown due to post traumatic stress disorder brought on by bullying. My parents didn't know what else to do so they had me sectioned. I'm not sure if I believe what I'm being told. I wonder what is real and what is not. Everyone seems normal and I suppose it makes sense that I am mad, I mean I felt like I was going crazy, and my parents are telling me that I am, so I guess I'll just have to accept it.

I give a weak half smile and tell everyone that I am tired and need a bit of time alone so I can rest and process what they've said. They all agree and start exiting the room one by one with Meg being the last to leave. The door opens slightly a moment later and Meg peers back through, "nothing is as it seems" she whispers and presses her finger to her lips.

# CHAPTER 7

I sit up in my bed thinking over and over what mom and dad said then what Meg whispered to me. I must see Meg on her own so I can ask her what she meant when she said nothing is as it seems. I need to know the truth and I think she knows what it is. I'm going to act as normal as possible around mom and dad which could be difficult given that I'm not sure I trust them now. I need them to believe that I do trust them though and that I think they truly only have my best interests at heart. Perhaps those people are not my mom and dad. They could be robots or aliens or something equally disturbing. All I know is something doesn't feel right and I'm going to find out what that something is.

I hate the thought that my parents are fakes and I trust Meg more than them, but I can't help how I feel. I can't trust them. I hear not-mom calling me saying that food is ready, and I must admit I am starving. It's only been a few days; well, I think it has but I am so hungry that I feel like I've got a hole in my stomach the size of a small crater. Why do I feel so hungry? If I am mentally ill and have been only here and in hospital, have they been starving me or is it that I haven't eaten since the other day when Meg, Chase and I had chips? One way or the other, I need food.

I make my way slowly downstairs and into the kitchen. My jaw drops when I see a glass jug filled with lemonade and bright red perfectly ripe strawberries along with many other sumptuous looking treats on the table. It's the same as the table in the place I think of as paradise that I visited yesterday.

I think it was yesterday anyway. I don't even know if my time in that place was in a dream, part of my supposed nervous breakdown or something else. Nothing makes sense now, but I decide to try not to think any more about it and just eat.

I feel a little reluctant to put any of the tempting looking food into my mouth as the last time I did that I fell asleep and woke up somewhere else and I'm not ready for that to happen again. I'm so hungry that I can't resist any longer and grab a jam sandwich, stuffing it into my mouth, chewing and swallowing as fast as I possibly can. The strawberry jam that fills the inside of the dainty sandwich made with thinly sliced white bread is so nice, not too sweet or overly sour, exactly like granddads homemade jam was. I guess mom had the recipe and copied it although this is not-mom not my real mom, I don't think so anyway. Maybe my granddad didn't really die last year, is he still alive? I try my best to put that thought out of my head as I don't want to give myself false hope that I might see granddad again, but the thought keeps creeping back into my mind, I can't stop it.

After eating most of the food that was laid out on the table, I am finally fit to burst so I get up and ask not-mom if it's alright if I go and walk off some of the food that I rammed down my throat. Not-mom looks around and stares at me for a few seconds, her eyes welling up with tears. "What's wrong mom?" I ask and she tells me she's just so glad that I'm finally getting better and looking more like her big girl again. I'm not sure that's all it is. She seems upset but not in a happy, relieved way, more in a woeful and desperate way. "So can I go out for a bit then?" I ask again. Maybe-not-mom says that I can go out but not to be long and to be very careful. It's not like her now to look that worried, she wasn't like that the last time I went out alone, but I suppose, if she is my mom, she's been through a lot lately with my illness.

Maybe-real-mom follows me to the front door and waits on the doorstep while I walk down the path to the gate at the end of the garden. I look back and she smiles with a sort of pained expression on her face, there's sadness in her eyes. I turn back around and leave the garden, stepping out onto the pavement and turning left towards Mr. Ramsbottom's shop. As I'm walking down the road, I see something fluttering around quite close to my face. I try swatting it away with my hand, but it just keeps coming back. It stops and hovers about a foot away from me in my direct vision. I can see it clearly now, it's a ladybird, a yellow one with black spots.

The ladybird starts to fly in the direction of the park, so I cross the road and follow it. When I get just past the entrance to the park the ladybird is right in front of me hovering like it has waited for me to catch up. It flies off again towards the pond. I again follow it wanting to find out where it seems to be taking me. I see the bench that Meg, Chase and I sat eating chips on the night that everything changed. As I reach the duck pond, I look across it to the little island in the middle. There was a small wooden house there before, but it looks different now, more like a much smaller version of the creepy old house at the edge of the field that the so-called party was at. I stare mesmerized by the perfect miniature copy of the house that I'm not even sure now was real. The tiny front door opens and a small boy, only about the size of a mouse steps out. He is tiny, like a little doll but I think he's real. He might need help as he's calling out to me. I think he is calling my name.

Even though his voice is small and squeaky, and I must listen carefully to what the doll sized boy is saying I can tell it's him, it's Chase. Fascinated by his tiny appearance, I don't listen properly to what he's trying to say at first but then he moves closer to the edge of the water and almost falls in as he's waving his arms around so much and jumping up and down. As I concentrate on his little face, I realise he's saying something. "Come here Alex. Come here quick!" Just as I'm wondering how I'm going to get across to the island I notice something in the water. It's moving upwards, out of the water.

I see it now, it's a bridge and it's completely transparent. I really do not want to use this to get across to Chase, I'm not a big fan of bridges anyway, they make me feel insecure, but this bridge is something else! There's no other way, short of swimming across to the island, which I am not doing, so I take a deep breath and exhale slowly before taking the first step.

The bridge appears to be made of thin glass so fragile looking that I feel it might crack and break at any moment. Fortunately, the glass bridge is a lot stronger than it looks and doesn't break but carries my weight until I am safely across to the island. I kneel and pick Chase up; I can hold him in my hand, but as I do everything starts getting bigger. I drop Chase as I can no longer hold him then realise that everything isn't growing and that I am shrinking. I am now shorter than Chase and the right size to fit through the front door of the house. "Quick, come on, this way" Chase says, and I look around to see a huge duck coming towards us. Chase runs to the front door with me close behind. He tries to turn the doorknob, but it won't budge. "Round the back" I say and start running around the side of the house towards the back door. The door opens before I get there so I run inside, narrowly missing being eaten by an enormous mass of beak and feathers. The door slams shut behind us and we collapse on the floor panting for breath after our scrape with death by giant duck.

It's not like it was before in here. The inside matches the outside this time. There is a real open fire that has burning amber cinders in it, an antique looking chair next to it and a small, very dainty and intricately carved wooden table, a glass filled with clear liquid on top of it. I walk across to the table and pick up the glass to study the mysterious, almost odourless liquid. I put the pretty glass adorned with pink roses to my nose again, I don't think there's plain water in it, it has got a very slight smell but not like anything I've smelt before, so I don't dare to take a sip. "I'll try it" says Chase, making his way over to where I'm standing. "But you don't know what it is" I say, concerned. "It could be poison Chase". "I'm pretty sure it's not poison Alex" Chase says, giving me a cheeky smile then taking a sip of the liquid that I couldn't face trying.

"It's vodka" Chase says putting the glass back down on the table. I don't know what vodka tastes like and I don't really want to know but I am relieved it is just alcohol and not poison or something that would change Chase into something different. I like him the way he is. There must be someone else here or there was someone here not too long ago because of the drink that has been poured and left on the table and the fire that's still glowing. "We should probably have a look around and see if we can find the person that was here, or still is. Maybe they'll know what to do" I say to Chase. Chase agrees that we need to find a way out of here and get back to our normal sizes and that maybe whoever was or still is here could help us, so we decide to check upstairs.

We make our way up the large wooden staircase that really is very grand (or would be if it had been more cared for), and then step up onto the long landing. Chase enters the first room he comes to, and I follow closely behind him. It's a bedroom complete with draped curtains, an elaborate dressing table and beautiful mirror adorned with pearls all around the edge. A massive four poster bed intricately carved into interesting patterns takes pride of place against the far wall. I walk over to the bed and touch the closest dark wooden post to me, running my fingers lightly over the carvings thinking to myself how long it must have taken whoever fashioned them to complete and how much love and care they've put into it all. I sit on the bed. It's so comfy and soft, reminding me of my own, much smaller and much less fancy bed at home in my little bedroom. I wish I'd stayed there now and not gone out for that walk.

"Come and have a look at this Alex" chase says, snapping me directly out of my daydream. He's by the window, looking out. I walk over to him wondering what it is he has seen. "What is it, Chase?" I ask, looking out of the window myself and cast my eyes upon what he wanted me to see before he has chance to answer me. There's water, as far as the eye can see but no giant ducks and I can't see the park anymore. No trees or land of any sort are to be seen for that matter. We are somewhere else. That same feeling, I recognise, that I've felt before a few times now washes over me, that lovely feeling of calmness and contentment making me stand so very still. I am not scared looking out of this window at the water but quite the opposite. I want to hold on to this feeling forever, to keep it. I feel like it's just for me and it feels right but I know I must turn away and lose it, at least for now anyway.

I force myself with all I've got inside me to turn away from the window and away from the best feeling I've ever felt and look at Chase. For a moment it's still there, lingering as I look into those eyes for probably a second more than I should have, then look away in embarrassment and it's gone, that special feeling. I hope I find it again.

I need to sit down, so go over to the bed and perch on the edge of the luxuriously thick mattress with Chase coming over and doing the same. "Where are we Chase?" I ask. "I don't know, honestly I don't" replies Chase. "Do you know how you got so small and how, when I touched you, I started to shrink?" I ask, hoping he might have some even remote idea about how we both ended up the size of my little sisters' dolls. "Sorry Alex, I haven't got a clue about that either" Chase says shrugging his shoulders then grabbing hold of my hands. "Look Alex, I'm not sure how we got so small, and I don't know where we are, but I swear to you, I'm going to find out one way or another. Everything will be OK". I know he's trying his very best to reassure me and I appreciate it, I do but I don't feel that confident. I just can't see how we're supposed to get off this island that seems to now be in the middle of nowhere. I tell Chase about meeting the little boy who looked so much like him a few days ago and tell him how I felt a connection to him. He looks at me like he wants to say something but doesn't and just looks down and laughs in a sort of nervous way. I decide it is best to change the subject as I feel like Chase is a little uncomfortable having a conversation about his five-year-old doppelganger.

Just as I am trying to start a different conversation there's a knock at the door. I stop talking and Chase and I look at each other staying completely still, frozen to the spot. I feel a shiver pass through my whole body then there's another knock. "Come on, we have to answer it" whispers Chase, "it might be someone who can help us find out what's going on or at least tell us where we are". I agree cautiously. We get up off the bed and start walking slowly, staying close to each other, out of the bedroom then down the staircase, every step we take making a creaking sound underfoot on the decent to the hallway.

We stand side by side facing the front door, just staring at it. "Maybe they've gone" I whisper to Chase then suddenly another, loud, urgent knock makes me jump back away from the door. "Chase looks back at me then steps forward stretching his hand out towards a long brass coloured key that is sticking out of the keyhole right below the doorknob. "Be careful" I say to Chase, worried about who or what might be outside the door. Chase looks at me and gives me a half smile then looks back at the key, stretching his hand back out towards it then turning it. I hear a click then Chase slowly turns the doorknob and finally opens the large wooden door.

# CHAPTER 8

I can't describe how relieved I am to see Meg standing there on the doorstep with Henry in her arms. Her hair is wet though and there's a rip in her t-shirt, this does not look good. Before I have chance to say anything, Meg steps inside and the hallway we are standing in darkens mysteriously. It's now very dark. Pitch black in fact, no light from the windows or the open door, nothing. "Is everyone still here?" I ask nervously with my fingers crossed, desperately hoping for an answer. Fortunately, both Meg and Chase answer me, even Henry meows. After a few more seconds of standing here in the dark, the lights suddenly come on. It's not natural light from the sun though, it's candlelight and it's dark outside.

"Are you alright Meg?" I ask, concerned by her dishevelled appearance. She explains that my dad had heard her try to warn me things weren't right back at my house. He waited until Meg closed my bedroom door then put a hanky that smelt vile over her nose and mouth, and she fell asleep. When she woke up, she realised she was in the house in the forest, she recognised it from before. The doors and windows were locked and after searching for a while for a way to escape Meg heard a meow coming from underneath where she was standing. She followed the sound down to the cellar but once inside, the door had closed so she was trapped there. She says that even though she was stuck in the cellar of a house in a forest in the middle of nowhere Meg felt calm, happy almost. That's when she saw Henry sitting on the opposite side of the room, close to the wall. She walked over to Henry who moved slightly to reveal a mouse hole in the skirting board. He sat there staring at her, not moving but meowing over and over until she lay on the floor to have a look through the hole then he stopped. Meg says she couldn't believe her eyes when, through the hole, she saw a transparent tunnel that looked like it was underwater. She desperately wanted to be able to walk through the tunnel, thinking it might be the only escape route and as soon as she tried putting her hand inside, she started shrinking until she was small enough to fit through the hole. She walked straight through the hole that only a mouse should be able to fit through and Henry followed her, he must have been able to shrink too. There were tropical fish swimming all around. Meg says it was a beautiful sight to see. She was amazed by what she saw in the tunnel. When they got to the end of it there was a valve that Meg turned then suddenly the tunnel disappeared, so she grabbed Henry and swam for her life until she made it to the surface then across to dry land, this island. Meg says she walked over to the house, still holding Henry, knocked on the door quite a few times and here we are.

So that dad is not my real dad then and I guess that means that mom was not-mom after all. I wonder who those people or things are and was Beth not Beth? It doesn't look like Meg knows who they are. I'm just glad she managed to escape and made it here to us. Now I'm glad that I did go for that walk after all and that I didn't stay at home.

"What was that?" I say hearing something coming from the back of the house, I think. "That was the back door" says Chase, "someone's coming!" We don't move. All of us stand still not daring to move then Henry jumps out of Meg's arms and runs over to a man who is standing at the other side of the hallway. I think it's the man who served us drinks the first time we were here, when the house was a normal size. "Please" the man says in a soft and friendly voice, "follow me." This man suddenly seems more than a bit familiar and it's not just because I've met him once before, I feel like I know him. The man starts walking back the way he came, into another room and we follow him one by one with me going first.

I gasp in shock as soon as I step into the room that I've followed the man into. It's the same as my granddads' dining room was. The table is the same as I remember, solid pine with a delicate but heavily embroidered tablecloth draped over it hiding scratches that I can just about make out underneath. There's the mahogany drinks cabinet in the corner filled with all sorts of different glasses collected from all over the country and a few different bottles of alcohol that granddad liked to treat himself to a small amount of now and then. Even the old piano that I used to try and play stands there against the wall majestically. If the room is a copy, then it's an extremely good one. The smell of sweet peas suddenly hits me and that feeling comes back to me once again, I feel calm and content in this moment. I take a seat at the table, as do the others then the man says, "let me begin."

The man pours each of us a drink of some fizzy liquid from a glass bottle before he says another word. Meg takes a sip, "oh it's elderflower, I love it!" she says smiling. I take a mouthful of the sweet, fizzy clear liquid and yes, sure enough it is flavoured with elderflower, the drink I always had when I was at granddads. "My name is Henry" the man says looking directly at me and deeply into eyes, then I see it, I know who he is. "Granddad?" I say, questioning what my own eyes see. "It is me, Alex" he says. I know it's a shock and very hard to believe but it's true, I am your granddad Henry, and this is my house.

I sit at the table, speechless, as does everyone else, apart from the young man that I now know to be my granddad who starts explaining what has happened. "I had to shrink this house to hide it from the people who were posing as your parents Alex. They are either not human or not from this time, that I am not sure of, but they are not your real parents which I'm guessing you already worked out for yourself and didn't need me to tell you. I do know that those beings seem able to change themselves to look like humans or animals. It doesn't appear difficult for them to do. I've seen them do it with my own eyes." I finish my drink and set the glass down on the table. I look back up and my granddad is how I remember him, complete with lines, grey hair and glasses. I jump up from my chair and race around the table throwing myself into granddads open arms. There's that wonderful feeling again but much, much stronger now I am in the arms of the best person in the world. Granddad kisses my head the same as he always used to and I look up at his kind, loving face finally feeling like everything is going to be alright.

"I'm so sorry you had to go through all this Alex" Granddad says looking down at me with sadness and tears in his eyes. "It's ok granddad. I'm happy now and I don't care what's happened." I say with a smile on my face, feeling safe, secure and loved. I give granddad another big cuddle then glance up at him and notice he's no longer looking at me but past me at something else. I look around and realise that to my horror we are alone, everyone else has gone. "They weren't real" says granddad in a sorrowful voice but expressionless, still looking past me. "You imagined them so hard Alex, subconsciously that they appeared just when you wanted them to." No, I can't have done. I can't have just imagined up my friends, they were real, I'm sure they were. Granddad says nothing but continues to stare at something that I can't see and then it hits me, and everything starts to make sense. I didn't have any friends that were my sort of age when I left school and I was so desperate for someone to like me, I needed a best friend. I was totally in love with a singer, a boy of sixteen who sang the most heartfelt songs, and I am a hopeless romantic. I always wanted a cat, but my dad is allergic to animal hair, so I had to make do with a rabbit that lived outside.

I start to see something in the direction granddad is still looking in. It's the yellow and black ladybird. It seems to be growing and changing right here in front of us. It's becoming a person, a girl with golden curly hair, it's Beth! I just stand still staring at her not sure if I believe what I've just seen happen then she runs over and throws her arms around me. I put my arms around my little sister, and we hold each other so tightly, neither one of us letting go then Beth looks up at me and says "goodbye, I love you" and she's gone, she's just vanished into thin air. "No!" I scream, falling to the floor with tears streaming down my face. "She had to go" Granddad says softly. "She did what she needed to do, she led you to me and now she's gone back." "Gone back where?" I ask, my voice shaking and feeling a mixture of sadness, longing and anger all rolled into one. "Your sister has gone back to reality" says granddad. "You didn't have a mental breakdown at all Alex but in fact you have powers, strong ones, you are very special. Your parents tried to keep your abilities hidden from you because they were trying to protect you from being different from everyone else, but it didn't really work, I think you've always known you are different; you didn't need telling. I'm like you. I also have some abilities or powers as I like to call them. I was able to turn Beth into a ladybird and put exotic animals in the paradise you walked through once. The tiger didn't wake up because it was never there, I put an image of it there to remind you of possible danger, to be aware of it and not to let your guard down too much. My powers aren't and never will be as strong as yours will become. There is great evil out there. There are evil beings that also have powers but use these powers to cause harm and destruction, they can change whole cities into whatever they want people to see and turn day into night. These things took your parents to an alternate reality, they are lost, and I can't find them, but you can Alex".

"How do I get there if you can't?" I ask granddad, trying my best to get my head around everything he has just told me. "You are stronger than you think my brave girl. Just follow your instincts and your heart, you will find them. You can save them" granddad says with a smile. "What about Beth, where is she?" I ask, worried about my sister. "I'm sorry Alex but Beth is in a place that I don't think even you can get her back from. I only managed to keep her here for a short time, she's in a place that doesn't exist yet, Beth is in the future and that is a dangerous place to be. You see the evil one's rule earth in the future and they took Beth from the present because she is the last-born human with powers, powers stronger than yours Alex, she has the power to change life itself and they fear her. They keep her locked in a white room with no windows and a glass roof." "I've been there granddad" I say "I remember the room. It was up a spiral staircase in a creepy old house on the edge of a field that I thought this house was when it was bigger." I'm so confused, and I sound crazy, even to myself. I'm almost in tears now. Those tears will be of sadness, anger and frustration if I let them fall from my eyes. "How do I get back there? I don't know how to get back to the white room granddad" I say desperately, needing an answer from him. "You do" granddad says gently and then suddenly, I feel like he's right, I think I know what to do.

# CHAPTER 9

I know now somehow that I can get back to the white room, but I don't know how I am going to save Beth as she's not even there yet. First, I need to get off this island. "Open the door Alex" granddad says, sitting back down at the dining table. "I don't want to leave you granddad" I say. "You must go, now. Don't worry I'll always be just around the corner." Granddad starts waving and seems to get further and further away. I look the other way and I am standing at the front door. I turn the knob and push the door open onto wooden decking and beyond it a beautiful white sandy beach. I step outside then turn around and the house is gone. I feel determined, on my mission to find Beth but regretful as I must leave granddad especially as I have only just been reunited with him. I hope he's right; I hope my wonderful granddad is just round a corner and not gone forever.

I walk across the decking and straight onto the warm, fine, pure white sand. It is perfect. I close my eyes and take in a deep breath of lovely salty and fresh sea air; exhale then open my eyes taking in the amazing scenery. I see a boat bobbing along on the calm shore a short distance away from me. The small sailboat is a beautiful turquoise colour, almost the same shade as the sea itself. There's someone standing up on the boat. It's a man and as I get closer, I realise who it is, it's Mr Ramsbottom. He's waving and calling out my name. "Come on Alex, we need to set sail" Mr Ramsbottom says. I step on board the small boat and say "hello". "Please sit down, you'll be safer if you do" Mr Ramsbottom says without looking up at me from the rope he is unwinding. I sit down on the small wooden seat which there's only one of and wonder where the captain of this little ship will sit. Everything is silent and calm as the last bit of rope is unwound, and the sail lashes up and out. A gust of wind comes out of nowhere, hits the sail and we are on our way, to where though, is a mystery that is yet to be revealed but oddly I don't mind that.

"I didn't know you could sail; in fact, I didn't even know you owned a boat" I say as the boat continues to be taken out to sea by the breeze. "There's a lot you don't know about me Alex, and this isn't my boat." Mr Ramsbottom says and looks directly into my eyes before looking at the ocean. "Who does this boat belong to then?" I ask. "In all honesty I don't know, it just found me, or I found it, I'm not really sure which way round it was." He says still looking at the waves. I get it, I kind of know what he means as things seem to just find me, or I find them too. I look at Mr Ramsbottom, he looks at me and we give each other a sort of knowing smile, like we understand each other. This feels so nice, the boat gently bobbing up and down on the calm deep turquoise sea which appears to go on forever. At this moment in time, I would be happy just to stay here, endlessly sailing, forever. Then I remember what granddad said and what I need to do, I need to get to Beth. My mind shifts and focuses on the task at hand and then everything becomes clear. It's like I've been asleep for a very long time, and I've woken up now.

"There it is" Mr Ramsbottom says. I look across the water and see an expanse of land that wasn't there before, like the fog has lifted and now it's in plain sight. As we get closer, I recognise the same shimmer that I have seen before. "How do we get through that" I ask then instantly remember how I got through before, I must find the gap. "Go on Alex, find your way in" Mr Ramsbottom says. He's not coming. I'm going to have to go through on my own. I step off the boat and everything turns grey. I look back but the boat is already in the distance, I can hardly see it now. I turn back around to look at the shimmer and start walking towards it. To my surprise, as soon as I approach the transparent wall, get close without touching it and look right, I am in exactly the right place and I see it, I see the gap. I slowly edge myself through the long thin gap which is only just about big enough to fit through, being extremely careful not to touch the sides which feel as if they would burn me in an instant. Once inside, everything is as it was the last time I was here. The sky is blue, the grass is green, and the air is a perfectly warm temperature, not at all like outside, which was chilly, dull and grey.

As I start walking across the lush, green almost springy grass I hear beautiful birdsong. I look up only to see a small multicoloured bird in the tree right beside me. I do like it here so much. Wherever or whatever this place is, it is near to perfection. I continue through the field until I hear a faint voice calling my name. I don't recognise the voice but want to find out who it belongs to and how they know me. There seem to be more trees around me now as I carry on walking towards the voice that is getting slightly louder, and I realise I am entering a forest.

There are huge blankets of delightful bluebells either side of me between extremely tall trees. I'm sure it is the prettiest sight I have ever seen and the fragrance the flowers are giving off is amazing. I hear the voice again, this time eerily whispering "Alex...Alex". Even though I am more than a little spooked by the sound of the voice I feel like I need to find out who this is. Perhaps they can help me find Beth. Whoever the voice belongs to might know where she is.

Up ahead is a very large and extremely tall tree that is blocking my path. The tree reminds me of the large apple tree that I used to climb in granddads back garden but much, much bigger. Some of the branches of this tree are low enough to climb up on and the apples look lovely and ripe. I'm sure they're just about to drop. As I walk up to the tree, I hear the strange voice again "knock Alex" it whispers this time. I think whoever said that means knock on the tree. It seems like a crazy thing to do, knock on a tree, but I guess it can't do any harm and I feel like this voice is my guide now, so I knock on the trunk of the towering apple tree. I stand back a little from the tree and see something being carved into it. The shape of a small door is cut into the bark by an invisible force and as soon as it's finished it becomes an actual door that opens instantly without me having to do anything else. The doorway is just about big enough for me to fit through, so I step inside the tree.

The inside is much bigger than the outside. There are stairs running all the around the circular wall of the interior of the tree that go up and up as far as the eye can see. As I get closer to the wall, I notice that it's decorated with wallpaper in a familiar print. I touch the wallpaper and feel the raised delicate tulip pattern embossed onto it. This wallpaper is exactly like the one in Beth's bedroom. I step back from the wall, now breathing more rapidly and starting to panic. How is this happening and where am I really? Surely, I can't really be inside a huge tree, can I? I sit down on the floor and take some deep breaths, trying to calm myself down, centre myself and think about my mission to save my sister.

There's nothing else in here, just the grey stone steps that run all the way around the edge of the round tall room like the steps inside the turret of a castle. I decide to start the climb up the staircase, needing to know what is up there at the top of this extremely tall tree, that is if indeed it is still a tree. I start making my way up the stone staircase and as soon as I do the floor drops away and the sides seem to be closing in on me. The wallpaper starts disintegrating until the whole place is just bare stone making it appear more and more like the inside of a castle turret. I've been here before. I know this place. I swear this is the castle that I've visited with my family in the past. The stone steps are the same and there are arrow slits instead of windows every now and again which make me imagine for a moment that I am an archer with my bow and arrow waiting to defend the castle from the enemy. I am up against an enemy, one I know nothing about, but I am pretty sure that sometime soon I will have to face them. There's now only one way to go. There's no way back so I continue onwards and upwards, climbing higher and higher not knowing what's in store for me when I eventually reach the top.

I'm sure these steps must be never ending as I still can't see the top and I've been climbing them for what feels like ages now. I'm getting tired and feel like I can hardly take another step, pushing myself to carry on, telling myself just one more, just one more when I reach the top, suddenly and step up onto a carpeted floor which I collapse in a heap on. I look down to see that I am lying on the thick dark blue coloured carpet on the landing at the top of the stairs in my house. The stairs aren't here though, neither are the doors, just the landing with the walls and the ceiling the same as they usually are. It's like I'm inside a rectangular box. As I look up, I see the loft hatch that has a pull-down ladder. If I could reach high enough, I could move the wooden board that covers the hatch and try to pull down the ladder so I can climb up and see if there's a way out through the loft. I look around and see something in the corner. It's a long pole. I get up from the lovely soft carpet and go over to take a closer look at the pole. It's quite long with a hook on the end. I reckon I can just about reach to push the board using the pole so I point it up towards the hatch, stretching my arm as far as it will go and standing on my tiptoes. The hook on the end of the pole just about reaches the loose board and as I push up slightly it moves enough for me to see the ladder. There's a small loop attached to the metal ladder that I should be able to reach with the hook if I can hold the pole steady enough and hook it. I use both hands to hold the pole as steady as I can and after a few failed attempts, the hook meets the loop and I pull the ladder down to the floor then start climbing up it.

I push the board to the side so I can get through the hatch and climb into the loft. There's a window in the roof but not much light comes from it as it looks like day has already turned into night. The night sky is perfectly clear, and the stars are shining more brightly than I've ever seen them before. The shimmer is still there, a clear dome that covers this place. I can just about see it above the treetops in the darkness. The moon is crescent shaped and bright like a beacon of hope in the sky above the shimmer which scares me a little more every time I look at it. There's no way I can get up and out of the only window in here, it's far too high and there's nothing to stand on apart from an old wooden chest that looks too heavy to move by myself. I step carefully across the bare floorboards to the chest. I wonder what could be inside, treasure, a map or answers to all the questions that have been whizzing around in my mind making me feel like I am crazy, that would be nice. The chest is quite large and looks to be made of solid mahogany. It's beautifully carved, reminding me of the four poster bed in the little house on the island. It's too dark in here to make out what the carvings say but there is writing on it in between swirling patterns in rows all over the chest. There is no keyhole so it can't be locked. I'm hoping I can just lift the lid up. I put hands on the lid carefully but firmly and lift. It opens, to reveal something I really wish I hadn't seen.

I inhale sharply and back away from the chest. What is inside was not what I was expecting at all. I feel physically sick. Inside the chest is a skeleton and it must have been there for years by the look of it. As horrible as the thought of it is, I feel the need to take another look at the skeleton. Maybe it's a morbid clue. Perhaps I was meant to find it. I walk back over to the chest and look down at the remains which I think are human. There's something shining in the moonlight next to the skull. I look closer and see that it's a locket. I reach down reluctantly being very careful not to disturb the bones and pick the locket up. I study it as best I can by the light of the moon. The pretty locket is silver in colour I think, and heart shaped with what I presume is a sapphire set into the metal. I open the locket up and see two photographs, one of a baby and one of me when I was younger, maybe seven or eight. Like I've been punched in the stomach it hits me, this was my mom's locket.

Tears stream down my face, I can't stop them falling, it's like someone just turned on a tap behind my eyes and I can't manage to turn it off again. It can't be. It can't be. It can't be. If I keep on saying those words in my head, then maybe they'll become true. It's no good, it's still there, the chest with my mom's skeleton inside. I feel sick again, my head is spinning, and I still can't stop crying. I feel like my heart is breaking into tiny pieces that will never be fixed now I know my mom is gone. I close the locket and hold it tightly in my hand.

After a while the tears finally stop falling and I look up to see the sun shining through the window. I loosen my grip on the locket and look at it. Mom was so upset when she thought she'd lost it. Granddad bought it for her after she had Beth so she could have a photograph of us both in it and keep us close to her. Mom's birth stone is sapphire, that's why granddad chose the locket for her. I open the lobster clasp that fastens the chain the locket is on and put it around my neck doing the clasp up. I open the locket back up to look at the photographs of my sister and me again and a light comes out from it which blinds me, so I close my eyes tightly.

I shut the locket and open my eyes. I am no longer in the loft but back in the white room with the glass roof. Sitting in an armchair in the middle of the room is my granddad. "Alex, you found it!" he says grinning. Granddad starts to laugh but I don't see what's so funny. "Where's Beth?" I ask looking around the large bright room then focusing back on granddad. He gets up and starts walking towards me without his stick he usually needs to help him get about. I'm getting a bad feeling about this now. I don't think that this is my granddad. "Beth's fine, she's at home with your parents, safe and sound. She's forgotten all about you Alex, it's like you never existed at all". "What do you mean?" I ask in a very small voice, feeling scared and intimidated. "You're not my granddad, are you?" He just starts laughing again then says "oh Alex you really thought your beloved granddad was still alive? Well, he's not after all. You see I took on his form to get close to you, so you trusted me, so you would do what I told you to, and it worked like a dream. It was the only way." The man who I now know is not my granddad says, grinning maliciously. "What do you mean, the only way?" I ask, now feeling anger starting to slowly bubble up inside me. "To get you back here of course" No, no, no, no! Beth was never a prisoner in this room like I presumed, it's me, I'm the one who is trapped here. "Welcome to the future" says the man and then disappears.

# CHAPTER 10

I sit on the polished floor of my shiny, stark white prison and cry. What am I going to do now? I've lost everyone, everything. How am I supposed to get out of here this time and what did that man mean 'welcome to the future'? I am so drained that I can't even think straight. I feel so tired. It seems like ages ago that got any sleep. I hear a whisper. Maybe I'm that tired, grief stricken and lonely that I am hearing things now. No, there it is again, someone's whispering my name. "Alex, don't give up." I hear whoever it is whisper softly. "Nothing is as it seems". It's Meg! The voice that's whispering to me belongs to my friend, she is real! I call out to her "Meg where are you? I can't see you". "Find me Alex, you know how to" Meg says. "But I don't know how to find you Meg, please tell me what to do" I beg her. Meg doesn't answer and I no longer feel her presence, she's gone. "Right" I say to myself with a newfound energy and will to survive, I need to escape, I must look for Meg. Think Alex, think. Ok so maybe I have got some sort of special powers, maybe the man that was pretending to be granddad wasn't lying about everything. If I have got powers, then how do I use them and what kind of powers are they? I concentrate and try to imagine a way out of this room. That could be it, maybe I have the power to make things appear that weren't already there if I just imagine hard enough. I think of a door. I think what sort of door it is and how big it is. I think about the colour and what it's made of. It's no good, it's not working. I'll try imagining something else, a person, Meg, I'll think about Meg. I think long and hard about how she looks and how she makes me laugh but it's no use, nothing happens. It must not work here in this white prison that I guess I may as well call home now.

Tears start to well in my eyes again and I think of Beth, how much I love and miss that beautiful little girl I am proud to call my sister. "Alex?" I look up to see a woman standing before me with long golden wavy hair, bright green eyes and a dazzling smile. It's Beth! She's an adult now but it is her. "Is that you Alex?" she asks. "Yes, it's me. That's you Beth, isn't it? Only you look much older than the last time I saw you." "So do you Alex" Beth says. I reach into my pocket remembering that I still have the little mirror I climbed so high to retrieve and stare at my reflection in it. Sure enough, once again I am older. I turn the mirror to Beth so she can see her own reflection to which she gasps.

It's a lot for a little girl to take in. Beth has just aged about twenty-five years in a split second and found that her sister has done the same. I start explaining to Beth that I have special powers and that these powers brought her to me. I tell her that I think she has powers too, she just doesn't realise it yet and all I know is that our powers can be used only for good. "I am being held in this room as a prisoner by someone who looks exactly like our granddad" I say hoping I am not completely blowing the mind of a four-year-old. She seems to understand and take in what I'm telling her a lot more easily than I thought she would have and then I realise, Beth not only looks older, but she is older mentally and so am I. "Ok so what do we need to do, how can I help?" Beth says looking at me seriously. "I don't know but most of what that man said was a lie. He said that you were trapped here but he just said that to get me here" I say thinking more about what he'd said. "Hang on, he said that this is the future so maybe we need to go back to the past and change something. I wonder if we can somehow make it, so this never happened". "Sounds like a plan if we only knew how to get out of here and then travel back in time" Beth says with not a lot of confidence in her voice. "I think it's something we need to do together. I'm guessing that's why it was you who came when I imagined you". "Wow so that's how I got here, that is amazing!" Beth says grinning from ear to ear, her eyes sparkling with excitement.

"Right, I'm guessing we need to channel our emotions, imagine something or someone you really care about and really feel your heart aching for them. That's how I got you here." I say smiling lovingly at my sister. "What about the apple tree in granddads back garden. The smaller one of the two that you used to put me on so I could sit on one of the lower branches while I watched you climb up higher" Beth says. "Yes, that's a brilliant idea, I think it'll work, in fact I'm sure it will" I say excitedly. I was so happy climbing that tree, looking down at Beth's innocent little face watching in amazement how high up I could go. "Beth, we need to imagine being in granddads garden, think of the tree." We stand opposite each other, hold hands then close our eyes. I think about standing in my granddads back garden looking at the smaller of the two apple trees. I feel utter happiness flowing through me, awakening all my senses, this is it, this is my power. Nothing happens. I open my eyes and look at Beth. She has her eyes squeezed tightly shut, this should have worked. "Let's try again Beth. This time remember how that moment made you feel when you looked up at me while you were sitting on the branch of the tree, the sun shining on your face and really feel the emotion, harness it and let it take you over. You need to give in to it totally and don't think or feel anything else, even for a second". "Ok" Beth says, "I can do this". I close my eyes and let pure happiness wash over me again. It feels stronger this time, the feeling inside me like I'm on the verge of exploding with overwhelming emotion. The energy I feel builds, more and more getting stronger and stronger and then stops.

I feel a light breeze on my cheek and open my eyes. I am here in granddads back garden standing on a branch of the apple tree. "We did it Beth, we made it back" I say. "Back where?" Beth asks. I look down at her and she is a child again. "It doesn't matter" I say, and Beth runs off down the garden to the house. We've gone back in time to before it all happened, granddad dying, the shimmer, the white room, it's all in the future, it hasn't happened yet.

I climb down from the tree and step onto the grass. I make my way onto the narrow path leading to the gate with the pink and white flowers all around it, open the gate and carry on down the path to the steps. The garden is raised above the ground floor of the house, so I have to walk down five steps to get to the veranda. I turn the handle of the painted, weather worn wooden veranda door, open it and step inside. It's nice and warm in here just like it always was, reminding me of the shimmer and how the temperature is the same when I am inside it as it is right now. I walk through the veranda to the wooden framed glass back door which is already open slightly and peer through. The door to the kitchen is wide open so I can see straight into it. There's no one in the kitchen but the amazing smell of hot apple crumble hits my nostrils, awakening my taste buds which water to the point that the sensation is almost painful, so I push the door open and walk in.

"Oh Alex, there you are. Finished your climbing then?" Granddad says as he comes into the kitchen from the living room. "The apple crumble's ready, come and have some while it's still hot" he says smiling at me. I run over to him and throw my arms around him never wanting to let him go. It's granddad, it's really him this time. We did it, Beth and I, we really did. We travelled back to the past and we found him.

I sit down on the sofa in the living room with a big bowl full of granddads homemade apple crumble and thick creamy custard perched on my lap. Beth is engrossed in a cartoon about puppies that help people on the small television in the corner of the room, so I start telling granddad, who sits down next to me, about everything that's happened. He doesn't look all that shocked when I tell him he died and someone tried to impersonate him, making me believe he had come back to life to make me trust him. He just nods when I tell him about the shimmer and being trapped in a white room, held prisoner by well, I'm not at all sure who. I tell him that I was able to shrink to fit inside a tiny house and imagined myself going back in time to get here. He still doesn't seem surprised. "I see" granddad says when I finish telling him about everything that's happened to me lately. "I always knew you had abilities Alex. Beth has them too. I was just waiting for the right time to tell you about them, to explain it all, when you were older." "But I needed to know about my powers granddad, you shouldn't have kept what you knew from me, you should have told me about what I can do" I say feeling disappointed that granddad felt that I was too young and immature to handle the truth. "I'm sorry, you're right, I should have told you, I can see that now. Please forgive me my lovely girl." Granddad looks at me searching for forgiveness, tears forming in his apologetic eyes. "Of course, I forgive you granddad, how could I not? I know you would have only had my best interests at heart" I say meaning every word.

"Well," says granddad pausing for a moment, "you have a much greater understanding now of what you can do. Experiencing something for yourself is far superior to someone telling you about it. You've lived it already Alex and you've come back to a time when you didn't know what you know now. You can do it all again but with the skills you've learnt and the powers you know how to use." Granddad's right, I know so much more now than the first time I was here, in the past that has become my new present.

"Do you know who he is, the man who pretended to be you granddad?" I ask. "I do not know his name, what I do know is that he is a human being but from sometime in the distant future. "I think he wants to harness your powers Alex and when Beth is older, hers too. My idea is that he needs the powers that not many people possess to keep him alive, keep him breathing, although that is just a theory. He is the last of all mankind and he is dying." "How did it happen; how does the human race reduce to just one person?" I ask, intrigued but scared. "In the future, human beings don't have facial features really and can morph into anyone they like from the past. Humans must stay inside the dome they created for themselves. They die very quickly the moment they step outside it. Humans gradually become infertile and one by one humanity starts to die out." Before granddad can continue telling me about the future, an old lady enters the living room. I've met her before. It's the lady who guided me through the forest to the table and young Mr Ramsbottom. "This is Megan" granddad says. "She's a friend of yours I believe." "Meg?" I look at the old lady in amazement, baffled by her appearance and how it was possible for her to be in the same place at the same time. "Yes, it's me Alex. You're wondering how I could have been in the same place at the same time as my younger self aren't you." "Yes" I say looking into her eyes, hoping for more answers. "That was me, as I look now, guiding you through part of your journey. The other me, the younger one was just a figment of your imagination. You wanted me to be with you, so I appeared to you when you needed me, as my younger self. I became real to you. This version of me, as I stand before you now is from the future. There aren't many of us left - the gifted ones. He summons people to him; I don't know how but I think it's because he needs them. Without our help humanity will die out" Meg says seriously. "So, he's not killing people?" I ask. "No" says granddad as he sits down beside me and holds my hand. "I think he needs power from the gifted ones to survive and I think he needs us alive and ideally captive, so he knows we are as close to him as possible at all times." "What about my mom?" I ask granddad trying to take in everything that he has just said to me "I saw the skeleton and here's the locket you gave her. Is my mom dead?" "No" says granddad squeezing my hand. "He would have wanted you to think it was her so you would put the necklace on, he knew it would make you feel like you were closer to your mother. Your powers are strongest when you are emotional and the pain from losing a loved one makes a person more emotional than anything else, that's why he put the chest there with the skeleton inside, he wants you to be emotional then he can use your powers. "So, mom's alive?" I say, tears already streaming down my face and landing in my bowl of now cold apple crumble. Granddad smiles warmly "very much so my darling girl. Everything that happened up to the night you entered his house is real, your childhood happened and is still happening. All your memories are real ones."

I am so relieved to hear that mom is alive and that what I think of as my reality is in fact real. Everything that has happened since the party in that house was all about him, a human being of the future who is not powerful enough to just bring me straight to him but instead must trick me into finding him, pulling at my heartstrings, leaving me completely vulnerable and open to suggestion. "What happens now he's lost me, now that I've escaped?" I ask. "The human race dies out; it has to Alex I'm afraid." Granddad looks down shaking his head. "I believe that the only way humanity can survive is for the people of the future to bring people from the past to them, people who are sensitive and empathetic. These people can really use their intuition and they have extra senses that most humans forgot how to use long ago. People like you are very special Alex." I've never felt particularly special just a bit awkward and after everything that happened at school, not very confident at all. Right now, at this moment in time I feel more confident than I have ever felt before. I am special, that's what granddad said. I have powers, I can use my intuition, I can sense what I should do, where to go, I just need to believe in myself, and I can make anything happen. I feel like I can do anything now, like nothing is impossible.

"So, I didn't have a nervous breakdown then?" "No" says Meg, "that was all him. He prayed on your insecurities and made you think of things that scared you. All the way along your journey you followed your heart and knew what you should do, with a little help that is" she says smiling and winking at me. "I'm so glad you're real Meg" I say, happy I really did find a true friend and she wasn't just a figment of my imagination. "Are we friends in the future?" I ask. "You'll have to wait and see Alex" Meg says. "The future is not yet decided. It can be changed. Humans doesn't have to turn into beings like the one you have already met. We can be different, better. You can change the world. Meg stares at me with a blank expression on her face and suddenly, like a bolt of lightning I feel an intense pain shoot through my head like the worst kind of migraine you can imagine. I screw my eyes up tightly and scream.

The pain is gone now. I open my eyes and look up at the ceiling of my bedroom. I sit up and throw the heavy duck down quilt off me, swing my legs round and over the edge of my bed and drop down onto the thick carpet below. I walk over to the door, open it a jar and peer out. I don't think there's anyone up here, but I can hear some sound coming from downstairs. I creep out of my bedroom being as quiet as I possibly can and slowly make my way downstairs trying to avoid the creaky bit of floor right at the end of the landing. "Good morning sleepy head." Mom says, well I think it's her, I bloody well hope it is this time. "Fancy going to the shop to get a loaf, I'm going to make eggy bread for breakfast." I run over and throw my arms around my wonderful mom squeezing her tighter than ever before. With tears of joy in my eyes I grab the five-pound note from moms' hand and head for the front door.

Once outside I take a deep breath of fresh air and breath out, exhaling slowly. I'm back. I have finally come back to reality, my reality. It feels good to be in the present, not in the future or the past but right here, right now. I am going to live in the moment, be present and mindful of everything that's happening at this precise moment in time because this moment won't last long, it's fleeting but it is important, as important as any other moment at any given time. I know things now, things that most people don't learn in their entire lifetime and I'm not going to waste that knowledge, I'm going to use it to the best of my ability and aim to be the best version of myself that I possibly can.

I've been walking and thinking about life, time and being a better person for about ten minutes and now I am here at one of my favourite places in the world, the little corner shop. I step inside to see Meg standing there. "Hi Alex" she says. "Oh, Meg you don't know how good it is to see you" I say beaming at her. "What are you like silly" Meg says and we both giggle. Mr Ramsbottom is here with his duster as usual, keeping the place spick and span, just as he likes it. "Hello young lady, what can I get you?" the old grey-haired shopkeeper says turning around behind the counter to face me. "Just a loaf ooh and a hundred grams of my usual sweets please but not the sleepy sort" I say chuckling a little. Mr Ramsbottom looks at me with a slightly puzzled expression then turns around and looks through the humongous and elaborate assortment of delights before finally finding the sweets that I'm after. He moves the ladder that leans up against one of the numerous shelves that have different sized containers sitting proudly on them, manages to just about retrieve the small glass jar of teacakes from the highest and furthest position it could possibly be perched upon and makes his way back towards me. "Why do you keep that jar in such a difficult place to reach Mr R?" I ask. "I don't, it's usually here" he points right behind him opposite the till. "I keep it here ready for when you come in um, oh yes that's it, A, A, Alex, I don't know how it got all the way up there." He shrugs and shakes his head scoffing and muttering something under his breath that I can't quite hear. Mr Ramsbottom takes a little silver scoop out from under the counter and measures out exactly one hundred grams of light brown, sugary, chewy sweets out of their transparent temporary home, pouring them into a small white paper bag then handing them to me. "That will be, um, two pounds please and just grab yourself the loaf before you leave." I hand the five pound note over to Mr Ramsbottom and wait for my change. Meg nudges me "Fancy coming to a party later?" she says winking. "I can't, sorry" I say thinking about what happened the last time I agreed to go to a party. "I'm spending time with my family this evening" I tell a slightly dismayed looking Meg. "Well, I think I'm going to go even though I'll have to sneak out. Chase is going to be there" she says grinning. I smile at her; she deserves to be happy. I pick up my change from the counter then say goodbye to Mr Ramsbottom and leave my favourite shop.

Meg and I walk back to my house together chatting and laughing like we did before. I get lost in the conversation and forget for a little while about everything that has happened recently then look across at the park as we approach my house, and the memories all start flooding back into my mind like someone just turned on that tap in my brain again. "Do you want to come in for breakfast?" I ask Meg, hoping to spend a bit more time with her now I've found her again. "I'd love to, but I can't, my dad's expecting me back in ten minutes, I've got to go. Bye Alex" she says and carries on down the road towards her house.

"Oh good, you're back" mom says as soon as I open the front door. "Let's get breakfast on, it's a late one but who cares hey" she says shrugging and smiling at me. I just smile back at my mom, so happy to be here with her and Beth. My little sister sits at the table colouring quietly while mom and I start making breakfast like we've done many times in the past, but I never appreciated moments like this back then, before. I do now. My thoughts turn to what the older Meg said about me changing the world. I don't know what that means right now or how I would even attempt to do such a thing but I'm sure if have confidence in myself, use my intuition and follow my heart the future, mine anyway will work out alright.

# CHAPTER 11

**2019**

I am so lucky. It's a beautiful day, a gentle breeze slightly cooling the midsummer air. I step out of a beautiful 1926 classic car dressed in vintage style lace, sparkly silver high tops and my hair in a loose up do. I hold on tightly to my bouquet of red roses that match my lipstick perfectly and look down at my gorgeous engagement ring shining dazzlingly in the bright sunlight. I can't believe I'm getting married! My dad steps out of the car and links arms with me. "Shall we?" He asks. I look at him, smile and say "yes, I'm ready." Filled with excitement and nerves I walk toward the doors of the village church with my dad by my side then I see something out of the corner of my eye. I turn to my left and see a cat, a blue one sitting there staring at me. "Henry?" I say, surprised. "Alex" says dad "who are you talking to? There's no one there." I let go of dad's arm and walk over to the cat that doesn't move an inch, it just sits there staring at me. I stoop down and put my bouquet on the ground then hold my hand out towards the beautiful creature. It lets out a meow as if it wants me to come closer, so I reach out further and touch the cat's velvety thick fur and my fingers sink into it. Everything starts to change, to go grey around me. Even the roses in my exquisite looking bouquet are losing their tone. I turn around to see that my dad has gone, just disappeared. Everything is silent until I hear a meow and then see the cat run off into the church. I follow it, pushing the large wooden door open more so I can get inside. There is a mirror hovering in mid-air where the vicar should be standing. The wedding guests are all gone, and it is cold in here, so cold I can see my breath when I exhale. I walk towards my reflection, feeling like nothing else matters in this moment. I am twelve years old again wearing a yellow playsuit and black hi tops at least that's what my reflection tells me but when I look down, I see that I am still wearing a wedding dress. I feel my hair then touch my lips and look at my fingers now stained with a red hue. The only similarity I have with my reflection is the high-top pumps but mine have been customized with dozens of crystals for my special day. My reflection winks and then turns around and starts walking away. "Wait!" I call out but my reflection keeps on walking until I can't see it anymore. What do I do now? Come on think, I need to use my intuition, all my senses, especially my extra ones. I should feel what it is I should do.

I turn around and make my way out of the church. I shiver, there's a cold wind now that whistles through the trees. I walk down the church path and see the car I arrived here in. The driver who brought me here is gone and, in his place, sits young Mr Ramsbottom. "What are you doing here?" I ask. "It's good to see you again Alex" Mr Ramsbottom replies without answering my question, "get in." I climb into the back of the car and close the door. This doesn't look like the car that I arrived in now that I'm inside. It's much bigger and looks modern with a completely panoramic glass roof. "Better hold on" my chauffeur says then taps a screen on the dashboard and we zoom off at high speed. I grab hold of the roof handle with one hand and the edge of the seat with the other as g force hits me in the face. "We're here" Mr Ramsbottom turns around and smiles at me. It only took seconds, but we are somewhere else already. I get out of the car, close the door and the bizarre vehicle speeds away into the distance.

I am back here, the place I visited a long time ago, the grey street. I turn around to see the tall thin house squashed between two shorter wider ones. It's the same house, the one from all those years ago. I walk up to the front door which opens before have the chance to knock on it. On stepping inside, I see two doors either side of the beginning of a long corridor with nothing but a dead end ahead. This looks different from the last time I was here, now I'm inside the house anyway. I wonder if there's a living room or an upstairs, this can't be it, just a hallway with two doors surely. The doors are both the same size, both made of plastic like the front door of many houses. The small amount of glass that creates a window in each door is frosted so I can't see through either of them clearly, but I can see something through one. I can't make out what it is but it's moving, and I get a bad feeling about it so move away and decide to try and open the other door. I walk across the hallway to the opposite white door and try turning the handle. It's locked, great. How do I get in with no key? Maybe this means that this isn't the door I should open after all. Even though I'm scared of whatever is behind the other door maybe I should take a risk and try the handle. Could the bad feeling I got looking through the window of this other door be about facing my fear of the unknown? Perhaps there is something utterly horrifying behind it that will eat me alive. Either way I feel I must open this door and take a chance. I turn back around and look at the opposite door. It's now wide open. I can see green grass, rolling hills and the sun is shining. I can feel the warmth radiating from it from where I am standing. Even so I turn back and try the handle of the door I am standing right in front of, the one that scares me. The door opens and I step into darkness and the unknown.

My eyes adjust a little and it's not pitch black anymore. I can make out that I am in another hallway, a seemingly endless one which is impossible to comprehend because this house looks thin from the outside but standing here now it seems as wide as a whole street, maybe wider. I should know by now that nothing is impossible and that things can change in the blink of an eye. Suddenly the lights come on and I am standing at the end of the hallway. There's no door to open this time and no brick wall either. I can see directly through the end of the hallway to what looks like the most beautiful scenery like the view from the open door in the first hallway. I don't understand, why could I not just go through that door into where I presume is the same place as this? What was stopping me?

As I edge forward towards the grass, I feel warmth and as I get closer it gets more intense until I stop and see it, I see the shimmer. I know what to do, I remember from the last time I found it. I need to look for the gap. I get as close as I can to the transparent wall, turn my head to the right and look down it. There's the gap, just wide enough for me to sidestep through into the sunshine. It's the same as I remember it, this paradise place that I know I can't stay in. I know that I need to be here right now, this is the right time, but I don't know when this time is. I've travelled through it, time, that I'm sure of. That's one of my powers, being able to travel through time. I learned that many years ago. I also know that I shouldn't travel to the past or the future unless it is necessary, vital for humanity to continue to exist. That's why I haven't used my time travelling abilities again until now. This must be extremely important, it's now that I know I must try and save humanity.

I have no idea how I'm going to save future human beings, but I presume I need to somehow stop them becoming featureless, resentful and cruel. One step at a time, I can do this but I'm going to need help. I need my friends Meg, Chase and Henry. I know they can help me. I know now that the cat I followed into the church was Henry, but I wonder where he went. He helped me outside the church, but I haven't seen him since I went inside. I see Meg all the time back in the present day, she's going to be my maid of honour along with my bridesmaid Beth. This makes me think of my fiancé Tom and my mind fixates directly and only on him. I stare into the distance, mesmerized by what I think I see. It can't be but it is, it's Tom and he's walking straight towards me dressed in his wedding suit. I run to him with outstretched arms ready to throw them around him but when I get to him, he passes right through me like a ghost. I turn around to find him, but he's gone. I nearly did it, nearly imagined him here with me, by my side but I couldn't quite make him stay. Maybe he can't be here, maybe he shouldn't be here, I don't know yet but I'm sure we'll find each other again, I hope so anyway.

I cast my mind to Chase. I haven't seen him since I was twelve. I wonder if he was real, perhaps he was just a figment of my imagination. It felt like he was real though, and Meg and I have never forgotten him so he must be. The feeling that he is here and that I need to find him is becoming apparent and starts getting stronger as I get nearer to the hills. There doesn't appear to be anything else here apart from grass under my feet and hills before me, not as far as the eye can see anyway. When I get to the foot of the first hill, I see that there's a small stream and a valley between other hills that I couldn't see before now. I walk around the hill that's in front of me and on towards the stream. The water is crystal clear, and I am gasping for a drink so kneel and cup my hands then scoop up some of the cool fresh water. As I bring my hands to my lips, I notice my reflection in the water. I am me, twenty-nine-year-old me but as I look down at my knees, I realise that lace no longer covers them and that instead of a wedding dress I am wearing a bright yellow playsuit. I look back at my reflection in the stream and see that it is different this time. I see freckles, mousey brown slightly fizzy hair and no makeup, I am twelve again. I am back in my own past now in myself but here in the future, inside this dome.

As I make my way further into the valley between hills as high as skyscrapers I see the most handsome looking chestnut coloured horse, with a long shiny brown flowing mane. As I make my way towards the tall and very muscular animal it looks at me then snorts and whinnies as if it's trying to talk to me. "Hello" I say holding out my hand to stroke the fascinating creature. The horse kneels so I can climb up onto it which I do without a second thought. I've never ridden a horse before, not even sat on one but somehow, I seem to know what to do. The horse stands up and starts to walk which turns into a trot and then quickly into a gallop. We are racing through the valley, following the stream, it's amazing. I feel so free right now. I hold on tighter to the horse's mane as we head out of the valley and into the field beyond.

We stop when we get to the gate. It's the same one, the one that I was guided through by Meg when I was here before, the one with the pretty flowers that reminds me so much of walking up the garden path at granddads. I lower myself down off the horse and look through the iron bars of the antique style gate. The perfume from the sweet peas hits me, it's so strong, so heady but beautiful and makes me reminisce about being in granddad's garden even more. I haven't seen my granddad for many years but still miss him and will never forget him or how he helped me.

The horse whinnies and nods as if he's telling me to open the gate so I press the catch down and push it open. As soon as I walk through to the other side the humidity hits me like a slap in the face and I instantly start to sweat. Feeling uncomfortable I consider turning back just for some relief, to fill my lungs with fresh cooler air. I turn around and the horse is gone. In the animal's place stands the boy I was trying to find. "Chase!" I say, standing in utter bewilderment on the other side of the open gate. "Is that really you?" "Yes" he replies, "in my human form at long last." "What do you mean?" I ask Chase, puzzled. "I did try to tell you before, but you couldn't understand me, horses apparently don't speak English" he says with a cheeky grin and a wink. "What! You were the horse?" I say, now more confused than ever. "Didn't you recognise my flowing locks?" Chase asks playfully as he runs his fingers through his hair still grinning at me. I start laughing and it feels like we've never been apart.

# CHAPTER 12

Chase steps through the arch of flowers and into the humid place, standing next to me. "Wow it's hot in here!" He exclaims using his hand as a fan without much getting much relief from the extreme heat of the unusual but familiar place, we now find ourselves in. "Have you been here before?" I ask Chase. "No, I couldn't get through. I needed you to let me in. I don't have the power to open the gate and anyway, it would have been difficult with hooves" he says. We both giggle and say no more about it, mutually understanding each other without the need for any more words.

Ahead in the distance is a castle. It's not like the one that I've visited before with my family, the one in the photo on my mirror, this one is more like a huge fairy tale castle. After a long walk through intensely humid rain forest complete with vines hanging from trees, monkeys swinging on their branches and the occasional sleeping tiger we finally reach the steps that lead up to the castle gates. The temperature drops rapidly as I put my foot onto the first step and in seconds, I feel freezing cold. It's a shock to the system as moments before I was dripping with sweat. I look back at Chase and see that snow now surrounds the castle. We make our way up the icy stone steps holding on to one another and being careful not to slip until we eventually reach the top and the castle gates. As we walk towards the entrance the large cast iron gates open automatically and it feels as if the castle itself is inviting us inside. Upon passing through the tall gatehouse a long rope bridge appears before us. It doesn't look like there's any other way to get further into the castle and we can't turn back now. I need to know if there's anyone here so somewhat warily, I step onto the first wooden slat and hold on to the rope either side. "Come on Alex" Chase says. I don't know how I didn't notice but he's already on the bridge, about six feet in front of me. "Ok just give me a minute" I say taking a few deeps breaths, trying to calm my nerves. I really do not like bridges, particularly ones like this that you can see through and do not feel safe at all. Right, I'm just going to take one step at a time, looking forward and not down, definitely not down.

Eventually I get to the other side. I don't know how; it was either sheer determination or the thought of not being able to do something that a boy could do and easily at that. I think it might have been the latter, no scrap that, it was the latter. I step off the rope bridge and onto a solid floor, collapsing in a heap at Chases feet, gasping for air, hyperventilating. I think about the last time I had a full-on panic attack, I locked myself in the toilet cubicle one horrible lunchtime, snuck out of school when everyone went back to class and ran for my life all the way home. This awful memory only makes me feel worse as I struggle to fill my lungs with the oxygen they so desperately need then everything goes black.

I open my eyes to see Chase's handsome face, those eyes like infinity pools that I wish I could dive into, and tread water forever look into mine and I find myself starting to fall without leaving the cold ground I am lying on. Maybe it's just the lack of oxygen to my brain for however long it's been since I got off that nightmarish bridge and nothing more. I turn away embarrassed at what I might be feeling and sit up then attempt to stand with Chase putting his arm around me to help me up. I compose myself and start walking along the stone floor of the castle towards a door that looks as if it is made of glass.

There's no handle. How do we get in I wonder? Do we have to smash it and if so, what would we smash the door with? I get closer to the door and reach out to touch it. As my fingertips touch the glass door it starts to melt. It must be made of ice;

not glass as I had thought. As soon as the ice has melted down to the ground I step through the opening, my boots splashing in the puddle the melted ice door has made and further into the castle with Chase following close behind. I glance back at the door, which is solid ice again, no evidence in the slightest of it ever melting. The room we find ourselves in must be the grand hallway. It reminds me of a museum I have been to, an extremely high ceiling, paintings covering the walls and a perfectly polished mahogany floor. "I'd love to take my shoes off and slide around in here!" I say, looking at Chase. With that he kicks off his trainers, "well let's do it then" he says grinning and whizzing off down the long and wide hallway. I laugh as I untie my boots then take them off and start sliding along the smooth and shiny floor in my handsome friend's direction. We meet in the middle and connect hands, our fingers locking around each other's then Chase starts pulling me one way, so I instinctively go the other until we are sliding around in a circle going faster and faster giggling as we go.

I hear footsteps and stop laughing. "Chase someone's coming, run!" We separate and start running towards an archway over to the right of the great hall. Past the archway is a stone staircase. "Come on, we have to go up" I say to Chase, knowing that this is the way. The way to what I do not know, all I do know is that I must get away from whoever was making those footsteps. We both collapse gasping for breath at the top of the staircase after what seems like a very long climb. I look at Chase "who was that?" I ask, just about managing to speak. "I don't know but I'm guessing you got a bad feeling about them too" Chase says, sitting up. I explain that I use my intuition to guide me and that I always seem to find a way no matter how impossible the situation appears to be. "You got me through the passage and into the future too, I couldn't get there by myself and believe me, I've tried many times. My powers are limited, unlike yours" says Chase looking me straight in the eye sincerely. I look away with slight embarrassment, feeling somewhat awkward. "What do you mean 'passage to the future'? Weren't we already in the future before the flowery gate when you were, well not quite yourself?" "That was Forever" Chase answers looking down. "It's like being in limbo, like the place between heaven and hell but between a second in time. Time just stands still when you're there, the next second never comes. You don't get older, and nothing changes. It's kind of perfect really, not to have anything to worry about. Once you are there you don't ever have to leave if you don't want to." "Oh" is all I seem to be able to say to that, like no other words are necessary. It kind of makes sense I suppose. Whenever I've been in that place, I have had feelings of calmness. I've looked at the most beautiful scenery and the air temperature is always perfect, not too hot or too cold but somewhere in the middle just how I like it. I am always tempted to stay there, in that place that I now know would be a permanent limbo. It is so appealing, the thought of being somewhere where you are safe and well, nothing is going to change, you don't have to think about the future too much and the past is filled with wonderful memories. I always know there is more though, I am never entirely satisfied there. I know I have something to do, someone to help. I have helped Chase turn back into a boy. I got him out of limbo land and got this far into the castle, so I've achieved something. There is still so much more to do though.

"Alex, look!" I snap out of my trance like state to see that Chase is standing by the window looking out. He's seen something. I stand up and go over to join him. I look out of the window across to a turret opposite and see a girl waving at us, it's Meg! "Meg" I shout out then hear footsteps coming up the stairs. "We have to go" says Chase. I look around for another way out but soon discover there is only one and that's through the window. Chase bravely steps out of the window which is not so much a window but more a large open space in the stone turret and onto the tip of a rooftop that slopes down almost vertically either side. I quickly follow him feeling I'd rather face my fear of heights and possibly falling to my death than what or who is coming up those stairs, getting closer and closer with every passing second. Once I step out onto the roof and find my balance, I find it easier than I thought it would be to walk across to the turret that Meg's in and before no time at all I am climbing through the turret window after Chase.

"Meg, what are you doing here?" I ask, more than a little perplexed. "I don't know" answers Meg, now her thirteen-year-old self. "I was about to do something, I can't quite remember what, but it was important, I know it was. The next thing I know I'm here, trapped in this tower." "It's a castle turret actually" Chase chimes in with a cheeky grin on his face. "Alright Mr know it all" I say nudging him and giving him what I think is a cute smile. He smiles back and for a moment we are lost, frozen in time, like we have forgotten where we are or what we are doing, like nothing else matters than this moment. I shake my head to pull myself out of this magical place where only Chase and I exist and realize I am seemingly trapped in this castle in the future being hunted like a fox by I don't even know what and I need to find myself and my friends a way out.

"There's no way out!" Meg says in a panicked voice. I tell her to try and stay calm and that we will find a way out. "We will get out, come on, help look for a clue that could help us escape" Chase says to Meg in a positive tone. We start looking closely at the circular wall in different areas at the top of this turret then the floor and out of the window. We find nothing. There don't appear to be any clues here that any of us can find in our quest to exit our current prison. As we sit down on the floor, the three of us with our backs to each other wondering what to do next I look up and see a bird high in the eves. It's not like any sort of bird I've seen before. It's brightly coloured red, blue and green like a parrot but I'm quite certain it's not one of those. Suddenly it swoops down and stands right in front of me, staring directly into my eyes without blinking. As the bird opens its long thin beak a strange squawking sound comes out. The bird steps closer, jumps up, perches itself on my leg and squawks again. "Hello there" I say as the others look at me and this fascinating creature with very curious expressions on their faces.

All the creatures that I meet somehow seem familiar and certainly seem to know me. This strange looking bird is no different. I wonder if it will turn into a person, someone I know like the horse did but then again that was when I was in Forever and not here. Maybe the bird will help us by showing us a way out of the castle. With nothing to lose and the slight chance of something to gain I ask the bird "how do we get out of here?" It just squawks again and flies right back up to the eves, perching on a very high beam. Well, that didn't help. Or did it? Looking up to where the bird is perched it seems different now, it's changing up there. I hear clicking, as if things are sort of slotting into place. The beams have gone now, there is no roof and I see a staircase starting to form, coming down to us and unfolding like paper that's been concertinaed tightly then let go. As soon as the last step hits the floor, I step on it and start the climb towards the open top of the turret, the others following my lead.

When I get to the top of the unusual staircase, I feel like I am standing on the very tip of the tallest mountain. The air is so thin, and I am struggling to breathe then I see what looks like the top of a slide a few feet away from me. I step closer to the edge of this small roof and look down. It is a slide, one that curls around like a helter-skelter. "Ok come on" Chase says before climbing up on to the top of the very long helter-skelter slide and then disappearing quickly down it. Meg goes next and then I am left at the top of the turret. "Alex" I hear voice say from behind me. I don't turn around to find out who said my name but instead climb up to the slide and whizz around and around all the way down it until I drop from the end and fall to the ground with a thud. "Ouch" I say, getting to my feet and brushing myself off with my hands. "He was there" I say looking at the others. "Who was it?" Meg asks. "I don't know, I didn't hang around to find out" I tell her but that's not true. I know who it was.

"We need to get away from the castle" says Chase but as we all look back around there is nothing there, the castle has vanished. I don't think any of us can believe that the castle could just disappear. Perhaps it was never really there in the first place, just a figment of our imaginations. None of us say a word about it and just start walking away from the where the castle was. I don't know where we are headed, what's in store for us next or when I'll see him again. I can't tell the others that I couldn't face seeing him again, hugging him, speaking with him then having to let him go. It hurt so much last time, and I don't want to feel that pain all over again. I must face facts; he will find me, and he will never give up. My granddad needs me but I'm just not ready yet. I don't say anything to Chase or Meg as I think it will be easier keeping how I feel to myself for the time being, I can't handle the questions that they will surely ask if I tell them the truth.

We've been walking in silence through fields of green grass for about half an hour when I see the shimmer up ahead. "We're at the other side" I say to my friends. "Already!" says Chase. "This place isn't that big then" he adds. It really isn't. I hadn't thought about it until now, but it does seem smaller than the last time I was here. "You need to go back now" I say to the others. "What, no, we're not just going to leave you here Alex" Meg says in a concerned tone. "You have to Meg, you too Chase. There's something I must do on my own, I can't leave yet" I insist, hoping that the two of them will understand and trust me on this. "Ok" Chase says. "Promise me you won't be too long though." Chase looks into my eyes seriously. "Promise me Alex." "I promise" I say lying to him and not knowing when I'd leave this place or even if I ever would. I show Chase and

Meg how to get through the transparent wall and tell them to look for the thin house. "When you go inside you will find two doors. You will have to choose one to open. Choose the one that feels right. Trust yourselves and follow your instincts, they won't let you down. I put my arms around Meg and give her a hug goodbye then Chase who holds me a little longer and a bit tighter. "Be safe" Chase says and smiles at me with sadness in his beautiful eyes. "Don't be long" Meg says. With that they slip through the gap and out of the dome, heading for the past. I just hope they choose the right past.

"Alex." I freeze, not wanting to turn around. "Alex" calls the voice again. I could easily escape through the gap, find the thin house and go through the door. That would be the easy option though and I know I can't take that one. I swallow hard, take a deep breath and turn around.

# CHAPTER 13

He looks the same as the last time I saw him. I throw my arms around my granddad and squeeze him tightly, tears rolling down my cheeks like a river running into a distraught sea of grief. "How are you here?" I ask, sobbing. "I can't be here for long Alex. I am only here to tell you that you must go back" granddad says softly. "Back to where?" I ask, puzzled. "You must go back to the year 2002. You need to start your life from age twelve again." Granddad explains that I must do things differently in my life to change what happens in the future. "How can I change the future? What do I need to do? I don't understand granddad" I say, perplexed. Granddad looks at me and takes my hands in his "you will just know my dear. Use your gifts." With that he is gone. "No!" I scream and fall to my knees, tears streaming down my face, my heart breaking into two all over again as I feared it would. I've missed him so much and now all I have left of him is this last memory of him telling me that I must save the world and I haven't got a clue how to do that.

After sitting on the grass for a while feeling the warmth of the sun and of the shimmer comfort me in my time of need, I contemplate staying here. It would be easy. I guess I'd never age, never have to make difficult decisions and maybe even see my beloved granddad again. I know I can't though. I know I must do what my granddad said and go back in time. I drag myself up to my feet and stand facing the transparent wall. I step forward, look to the right and sidestep through the gap. There's no going back now, I must push forward so I head towards the thin house. After about an hour of searching for the unusual looking house, I realise that it's not here. Where could it have gone? How can a house just move or disappear and how am I going to get back to the past?

I stop when I hear a meow. It's faint at first then it gets louder as I take a few more steps. "Meow" I hear it again then stop and look down. There's a manhole cover right underneath me; the sound is coming from below it. I stoop down and try to pull the cover off the hole but it's too heavy for me to lift. I try again but it won't budge. I kneel in front of the manhole cover and think about how I've changed things before to help me and imagine the cover is made of wood instead of metal. I close my eyes then open them again. That's it! Just like that the cover is now made of wood and is light enough for me to lift off with ease. I slide it off and put it to one side then look down the hole. It's dark down there but I can just about make out the top rung of a ladder just a few feet down inside the hole. "Meow" it's louder this time and it is coming from the bottom of this dark hole. "Oh well, here goes nothing" I say out loud and reach down with my foot until I feel the first rung of the ladder. On my climb down I hear the cat's meow again but this time more in the distance and with an echo after it. The bottom of the hole is dimly lit by a single candle in a holder sitting on a tall thin table. I pick up the candle and hold it out in front of me so I can look around. I see a small hole in the wall near the floor and walk towards it to take a closer look. I place the candle on the cold stone floor as close to the hole as possible and lie down so I can see through it. It's a tunnel, but one that's obviously far too small for me to squeeze through. I imagine hard that I am as small as a mouse. Using all my emotions, tears coming to my eyes and feeling my heart beating so fast and swelling like it is about to burst I close my eyes tightly and hope.

I open one eye then the other to see to my amazement that I did it! I am now as small as a mouse and easily able to walk straight through the tunnel. As I make my way through the now enormous and fortunately well-lit tunnel, I hear the cat meow again. "Henry, is that you?" I call out, my voice echoing all around me as the sound hits the inside of the underground passageway. I take one more step and there he is, sitting ahead of me just before the tunnel forks in two. "Which one do I choose?" I ask the fluffy blue cat. He just sits and purrs loudly, so I guess this means I must decide which way to go by myself. I wonder why I always end up having to make a choice wherever I go. Nothing is ever simple. I hope I make the right choice this time. I know now that I need to use my intuition at times like this so after a little consideration then entirely going with my gut feeling I choose the left tunnel.

As I take my first step into the unknown of this new tunnel everything changes. I am now in a room with shelves all around it and right up to the ceiling. The shelves are piled high with white cardboard boxes. I approach the nearest shelf to me and lift the lid of one of the boxes. There are sweets inside, hundreds of them, all different shapes and colours. I realise that I have somehow found my way into the stockroom of Mr Ramsbottom's shop. I don't know how the tunnel could possibly have become this room, but I wonder if the shop is behind the door that is now in front of me. I do hope it is. I am longing for the familiarity of the corner shop that I know so well and old Mr Ramsbottom smiling and joking with the customers. I have loved being twelve years old again and I'm kind of hoping that I don't change back to twenty-nine when I open the door, but I feel that it might happen or that something will anyway. Oh well, here goes. I turn the handle slowly then pull on it, so the door opens just enough for me to see what's behind it. It does appear to be my favourite shop, just like it's always looked, there's the counter and the old-fashioned till. Just then I hear a meow and turn around. Henry is sitting on one of the shelves opposite just staring at me and not blinking. I turn back around to see Mr Ramsbottom standing there with his back to me. I hear something drop behind me then the shopkeeper turns around.

He has no features on his face, it isn't him, this isn't right. I shut the door and turn a key that's now in the lock. I look back at Henry and see that the shelves are gone, and another tunnel has appeared behind him. Henry runs off into the tunnel and I follow him, my heart pounding so hard it feels like it's about to burst through my chest at any moment. After a few minutes of running as fast as my legs can carry me in near darkness I slow down and stop when I see the tunnel I am inside coming to an end and the opening of another tunnel before me. The tunnel in front of me must be the one I came through to get here in the first place right after I managed to shrink myself to the size I am now. There is another tunnel as I look around to my left which must be the tunnel that was on my right before I entered the one that I'm in now. I guess I'll have to try that one now as it is the only one that I haven't explored yet. I can't see Henry, but I really hope that he's gone the same way that I'm going. He's helping me so much as he has always done, and I feel like I need him more now than ever. I'm out of breath after so much running that I slow down to a steady walking pace thinking that even if that thing got into the storeroom and followed me inside the tunnel that I might have lost it now I've gone this way. I see light up ahead and realise as I get closer that in fact it is sunlight.

I step out of the tunnel and into the open. With long green grass underfoot I see that I am in a field. I see the creepy old house and the forest beyond it. I wonder when this is, what time, which date? Then I see my friends Meg and Chase. They look the same as they did when we went to the party that turned out to not be a party after all on the night that everything changed. I call out to Meg and Chase, but I don't get a response to me shouting their names. I call out again, as loud as I can but still, they don't seem to hear me. I don't understand why my voice is silent to them when I can hear it myself. Why aren't they listening to me? I'm not that far away from them.  It's like I'm not here and maybe I'm not.  I don't know.  I don't know anything anymore.

I sit down on the grass crossed legged with my head in my hands as I have been doing a lot lately.  What to do now I wonder. Think. Think. Why can't they see me? Why am I here now, in this time?  I know I need to start over, to do something differently or try to change something but why tonight?  Then it occurs to me, maybe we weren't meant to meet, Meg, Chase and I or maybe they just weren't meant to meet me.  Could it be that I am supposed to see where they are going and what they are doing at this particular moment in time but that they are not supposed to see me?  I think that if we meet now all over again something will happen that shouldn't.  I think I already knew this deep down that's why I subconsciously made them not hear me when I called out their names.  I'm not sure we are ever meant to meet and to become friends, but I do hope we are, ever so much, sometime in the future.  I wait until Meg and Chase go inside the house and get up off the damp ground.  I am going to go home.

As I start walking towards the cottage that I grew up in I think about whether everything will be the same as it was when I was twelve before.  What if I'm still at school and I never left.  Am I still being bullied?  What if, this time I haven't told anyone yet and I haven't left school to be home educated.  I really hope I did pluck up the courage to tell my mom how bad it got for me with those awful girls.  I don't know if I could go through what I went through before.  Well anyway it looks like this is it.  That I really am starting my life over from age twelve.  I try to put my concerns to the back of my mind as best I can and make my way back to the place I grew up in before.  Now I am going to grow up all over again starting from this moment.

"Alex!" Mom runs out of the house and down the garden path towards me as I get to the front gate.  "I was so worried about you.  Where on earth have you been?"  She says throwing her arms around me. "Err. Sorry mom. Time just ran away with me; I didn't mean to be so long" I say hoping that that's enough of an explanation. "You've been gone over an hour, and you said you would only be ten minutes." Mom really does look concerned now. Apparently, I was only meant to be popping to the shop for milk so mom could make pancakes. I must have gone back in time slightly further after I left the field. It was evening then but now it is morning, THE morning, the one before it all happened! I put my arms around my wonderful mother and cuddle into her feeling safe at last. She tells me she loves me then says that I should let her know if I'm going to be at all late back in future. I tell her I will do without knowing if I am actually telling her the truth. I love her too, so much. I'm just glad to be home.

When we get inside the house everything looks the same as it always was. I tell mom that I am just going to the toilet and run upstairs to check out my bedroom. It's just how I left it. The same cover with pictures of cute kittens all over it encases my wonderfully warm and heavy duck down quilt which lies in a slightly skewed fashion on my bed. The same pictures of teenage boy celebrities are there stuck on each of my walls like a collage of youth and vitality itself and the photo is still there, stuck on my mirror in precisely the same place I put it. I walk over to my dressing table and pluck the photo of myself and my family from the corner of the mirror. It's the same as it always was. I stick the precious photograph back on to the mirror and breathe a huge sigh of relief. It does look like my life is just like it was before at the same moment in the past which has now become my present. Something else has to change between now and when I am almost thirty years old and not just Meg and Chase not meeting me today. There will be another alteration I will have to make to my teenage or young adult life. I just don't know what it will be or when it will happen.

# CHAPTER 14

Tonight is the night! My party is happening later, and I am so excited, it's not every day a girl turns twenty-one! Life has been kind to me since the day I went back and became twelve again. Certain things have been different from the way they were the first time around because I didn't make friends with Meg or Chase as we never even met but I made new friends and have tried to forget about the cool girl and the cute boy with those eyes. I have got on so far with my life in general in the best way that I could. To be honest, I struggle to remember my previous existence, the one before I went back. It's like I have half memories or like it was all a dream and that other life which I am sure I lived wasn't even real. The best way I can really explain those memories is that they are covered by thick fog, and I can't see them properly, even thoughts of my old friends are too far away to reach clearly. I guess that it is for the best. I can try to put it all behind me and live in the here and now, until I find out what I need to do in the future, that is.

I lie down on my bed and for now think about what tonight will be like. I wonder if I'll meet anyone at the party, anyone that I don't already know and someone of the male variety preferably. I hope so anyway I think, smiling to myself. I haven't had a proper relationship romantically yet, not because I haven't wanted to, I just haven't met anyone special enough to get further than a few dates with. All my family are coming to the party, even my great uncle Albert who is nearly ninety. My friends from the home education community that I've known for years will be coming as will all my friends from university.  There should be quite a large crowd in the village hall tonight. I am very lucky. Unfortunately, my dad won't be at my party.  He passed away five years ago at the not very old age of fifty-six.  When he was dying, I had hoped I might be able to use my abilities to save him, but I now know, all too well that I don't have that kind of power and that I can't just choose who lives and who dies.  I don't know how I'm going save all of humanity if I couldn't cure my dad's cancer, but I suppose it doesn't work like that and that the two things are not the same.

I wipe the tears that are rolling down my cheeks away with the back of my hand and sit up.  Enough of this depressive stuff, I need to decide what to wear tonight.  I get off my bed and go over to the wardrobe opening both doors when I get there.  I've already whittled the choices down to three outfits.  There's a long midnight blue silky dress with skinny straps, a short pink A-line dress with long sleeves and an emerald green sleeveless jumpsuit.  I love all three outfits each for different reasons and my black pointy kitten heel shoes go with all of them. Hmm, what to do? Just then Beth comes into my room. "Alex, does this look ok for tonight?"  She asks looking absolutely stunning in a knee length slinky black strapless dress that makes her seem way older than her fourteen years.  "You look great sis, definitely the right choice" I say to Beth, really meaning it. Despite there being such a big age gap between us Beth is my best friend.  We tell each other everything and were there for each other when dad died.  I really don't know what I would do without my little sister. "What do you think I should go with then, out of these three?" I ask pointing the outfits out to Beth. "The blue" she says, "no, the green." She pauses, "but the pink one is so pretty!" "Well, you're a lot of help" I say sarcastically and we both giggle. "Ok. I'm just going to with the blue" I say, having to decide. "Good choice Lex, that's the one I'd have gone with" my sister says with a wink and a cheeky grin.

After having a nice long hot shower then putting on some

mascara and a slick of dark red lipstick and doing my best to blow dry my slightly frizzy hair I slip into the long blue dress. I look at my reflection, "you don't scrub up too badly" I say to myself out loud. Mom calls me from downstairs saying the taxi is here. I take one final look in the mirror, grab my black sequined clutch bag then make my way downstairs and out of the front door, closing it firmly behind me.

Outside is car that doesn't look like any taxi I've ever seen before. It's a stretch limousine! "Surprise!" mom says as I stand outside the front door staring open mouthed at the swankiest car I have ever clapped eyes on. "Wow mom" I say as I open the front gate, astounded by what she's done for me to make my birthday even more special considering money can be tight sometimes. I tell my lovely mom that she didn't need to do this but of course she tells me not to be silly and that I deserve to be treated, especially on my birthday. I am so excited and if I'm honest, a little overwhelmed as I climb into the extra-long white car with blacked out windows. Inside there are tiny fairy lights all around the roof that remind me of fireflies. It's more like a memory, like I remember seeing this before, but the lights were alive and dancing around me. Maybe it was a dream. I try to shake the thought of the fireflies out of my head. I have lots of very vivid dreams. I have done for years now, nine to be exact. I have dreams about houses with interiors that don't match with their exteriors and dreams of being older and standing on a cliff top looking out to sea. I even dream about eating sweets that make me fall asleep. They all feel so real when I first wake up then fade a bit throughout the day. I don't know what these dreams mean or whether in fact they mean nothing at all and they are simply pointless dreams, just my overactive imagination calling on me while I sleep. What I do know is that every time I wake up, I feel a sense of calm wash over me which turns into fear for a split second before turning back to calm once more.

On our journey to the church hall, mom, Beth and I sip cheap fizzy wine out of champagne flutes and reminisce about the past. We talk about all the great times we had with dad and agree that he was the best husband and father anyone could ever ask for. Mom has tears in her eyes as she talks about dad. She still loves him so much, as much now as she always did and misses him immensely. My parents met when my mom was the same age as I am now and were married a year later. They had never really been apart since then and I know mom has struggled without dad but always has put on a brave face through her grief. We all laugh when I bring up the time that dad put salt instead of sugar in a cake he had made for pudding one Sunday and not to hurt his feelings, mom and I tried to eat it and not say anything and Beth being so little spat a mouthful of it straight back out into her hand saying "urgh, that's yucky!"

After tears and laughter, both in equal measure over memories of dad, and plenty more sips of fizzy fruity alcohol we pull up outside the church hall. The church hall itself is so pretty, picturesque in fact, as if it's been plucked from a postcard and placed in our small part of the world. I hope that I get married here one day, when I meet my Mr. Right. Looking at the church opposite and with that thought firmly etched into my mind I get an overwhelming feeling that I've been here before. I can picture myself in a wedding dress so vividly that it's like an actual memory. I must have dreamt it, that's the only explanation I can come up with. I try and let the thought of getting married slip out of my mind and just think about all the fun I'm going to have tonight as I turn around and walk towards the doors of the church hall.

There's a large banner with 'happy 21$^{st}$' on it and as I make my way through into the function room, I see it has been decorated from floor to ceiling with balloons, streamers, confetti and yet more banners. "Wow!" I say to mom. "This is amazing, thank you so much!" Mom tells me that everyone chipped in to pay for the hiring of the hall, the decorations and the sumptuous array of buffet food I see over to the right of me that covers three whole huge tables. This is going to be the best night, I know it. The DJ starts playing my favourite song and Beth grabs my hand, pulling me straight to the dance floor. We grin at each other then start dancing, spinning around and around giggling until the music stops abruptly and the lights in the hall flicker off then on again. I look all around the room. Everyone has gone.

The hall is completely empty, I am alone. Gone are the guests, the sumptuous looking buffet food and the elaborate party decorations. I look around for any kind of explanation as to what has just happened but there's nothing, no clues, just an empty room. A strange smell hits my nostrils, and I can't decide whether I like it or not but it's not like anything I've ever smelt before. The fragrance is not too sweet, not too floral and makes my nose tingle as I breathe it in. Then I taste it. A most foul taste hits the back of my throat and no matter how much I cough or swallow it won't shift; it's absolutely disgusting. Just as I think I might be sick the vile taste leaves my mouth as instantaneously as it appeared and I am left with a much more palatable, deliciously sweet one in its place, a familiar one, a mixture of toffee and coconut. Memories of my childhood flood back as I stand still on the dance floor. This flavour out of all the flavours I have ever tried is my all-time favourite. It doesn't sound that amazing or remarkable but trust me, it is the taste sensation that is a sugary and hard but chewy teacake, the best sweet ever!

"Enjoying that?" says a voice coming from behind me. I turn around to see who it is. To my shock and delight I discover Mr. Ramsbottom standing right in front of me. "I know you don't know what this means right now Alex, but you will. Just remember the scent" Mr. Ramsbottom says then vanishes into thin air right before my eyes. The lights here in the function room flicker off and on again then the music starts playing and in a split second everything is just as it was, the guests are all here, the table has an abundance of food on it once again and Beth is standing before me with a puzzled look on her face. In a haze of confusion, I go and sit down by the wall on one of the plastic chairs that have been set out all around the edge of the room. I am not at all sure what just happened, but I do know something, I really need a drink. As I am about to get up and make my way over to the drinks table a glass is handed to me. I instinctively take the heavy cut glass goblet and touch the fingers of the person who offered it to me. The hairs stand up on the back of my neck and my whole body tingles. I've never felt anything like this before. Electricity flows through me and I feel more alive than I have ever felt before. I look up and cast my eyes on a beautiful young man with bright blue eyes and dark brown hair. After staring at each other for what seems like an eternity but must only be a few moments, I feel butterflies in my stomach fluttering around and doing somersaults. Embarrassed I look down and take a sip of fizzy pink liquid. It tastes sublime, this wine, it's the only alcoholic drink I really like, not too strong and quite sweet. I'm not a big drinker but I really like this. How did he know that out of the huge variety of drinks to choose from that this wine was what I would have chosen myself? Thinking about it there were only plastic cups on the drinks table, I'm sure of it so where, I wonder, did this unusual glass come from? I look closely at the large goblet and see that there is a picture cut into it. It's a picture of a house with a chimney. I recognise it, I don't know how but I just do. I look up and the handsome stranger is gone. I stand up and look around the hall, but I can't see him anywhere.

Was that mysteriously charming man just a figment of my imagination? Surely, he couldn't have been. He gave me this glass and the way he made me feel when I looked into his eyes, I've never felt that way before. I decide to get some air so make my way to the back door of the hall, push on the bar that acts as a handle on the door and let myself out. Once outside and standing in the dark, I take some deep breathes which hurt my throat a little as the night air is chilly. I know what I need to do. I must find the man who gave me the glass. I have to know who he is.

After going back inside the church hall and to the party, I chat to friends, dance and eat bits of food like I am supposed to, but it just feels like I'm going through the motions and not really enjoying myself as I know I should be. As the night draws to an end and the DJ plays the last song, wrapping up his set, I actually feel quite excited to take all my presents home. I'll open them first thing in the morning when I get up as it's quite late now. I can't forget about what happened earlier though. I know my electrifying but fleeting encounter with that gorgeous stranger was in some peculiar way significant.

The next morning, I wake with a start. I had that dream again, the one where I escape from someone or something never finding out who or what it was that I was escaping from. In a cold sweat I throw my quilt off myself, get out of bed then go and open the window to let some air in. "Morning" I hear as I breathe in the cool fresh air. It's the postman, he's walking up our garden path holding some post and carrying what looks to be a full bag on his back. "Hi" I say to the postman to be polite then remember I have presents waiting downstairs for me. I quickly put on my huge fluffy grey dressing gown and rush downstairs.

"Good morning sleepy head. Coffee?" Mom says smiling. "Yes please" I reply, yawning. I walk into the living room and see that my presents have been placed next to the fireplace, presumably so I can sit in my favourite spot on the soft multicoloured rug and open them. There are so many here, all wrapped with different coloured paper, ribbons and bows, I feel extremely lucky and well-loved right now. Bursting with excitement like a small child on Christmas morning I start the mammoth but fantastic task of unwrapping all my presents.

I am almost done. Before me, all laid out neatly on the rug is an array of wonderful gifts including perfume, a jewellery box, clothes, bath bombs, bottles of wine, make up and quite a few other bits and bobs. There is only one present left, it's quite small, wrapped in silver paper and tied with a bright pink bow. I can't believe I didn't notice this gift before, it's so pretty, I can't wait to see what's inside! I undo the bow and the wrapping falls away to reveal a small wooden box. On the lid of the box is an engraving of a house. It's the same house as I saw on the side of the glass goblet from the party last night, I'm sure of it. I open the box and see to my astonishment a shiny silver key pendant. One single sapphire set towards the top of the key shimmers in the sunlight that is streaming in through the front window. A feeling of pure serenity drapes itself over me, enrobing my whole body with joy then seeping through every fibre of my being like an invisible force of nature has captured my very soul while I sit looking at the key pendant, totally and utterly mesmerized by it. The longer I look, the more I seem transfixed, like I cannot possibly look away from my beautiful but mysterious gift. "Alex." My mom's voice snaps me out of my tranquil trance-like state, and I drop the wooden box, the pendant falling out onto the floor. "Are you ok?" Mom asks me with a slightly concerned expression on her face. "Yes, I'm fine thanks mom" I lie and pick up the pendant, putting it safely back in the box.

After taking all my other presents up to my room with moms help, I sit on my bed holding the only one that has left me feeling like there's more to it. It can't just be a normal piece of jewellery, not when it made me feel like that, not to mention the fact that I have no clue as to who it is from. I take the shiny key out of the box deciding that I must wear it but how can I when I don't have a chain to put it on? I remember that mom has a necklace that she hasn't worn for a while so go to my mom's bedroom to ask if I can borrow the chain. I leave my bedroom and walk across the landing to mom's and as I get closer, I see that mom is sitting on her bed looking at something she's holding in her hands. "Hi mom, can I ask you something?" I say standing just inside her bedroom by the door. Mom looks up at me smiling, "Of course you can." I walk into mom's bedroom and sit down on the bed beside her then I look down at what she's holding, a locket on a chain. "Your granddad bought me this after your sister was born so I could put a photograph of you and Beth inside it. I haven't felt like wearing it since granddad passed away, so I keep it in the box it was given to me in" mom says then picks the box up from beside her on the bed. The small wooden box is the same as mine. It has the same picture of the house with the chimney carved into the lid. I don't say anything about that to mom not wanting to upset her or confuse things, so I just ask if she minded if I borrow the chain she's holding for the time being. "Of course, I don't mind my darling, I'd be happy to let you wear it, in fact why don't you keep it. I doubt I'll ever feel like putting the necklace on again." I don't know what to say to my kind and caring mother, so I just give her a big cuddle and take the long silver chain leaving her to put the locket back in the box and then safely back in the drawer of her bedside table.

Back in my room I take the key out of the box that sits on my dressing table and thread the end of the long silver chain that my mom gave me through the open part of it at the top. Holding the small lobster clasp in one hand and the end of the chain in the other, I reach round to the back of my neck and hook one of the links. I feel a charge of something indescribable shoot through me at lightning speed and instantly I feel different, wiser somehow, I think, like I know more about life than I knew before. Something has changed in me now I've put the necklace on.

"I'm just popping out for a bit" I shout whilst running downstairs and whizzing quickly out of the door. I need to get out of the house. I need to breathe in some fresh air and digest everything that just happened with the key and what happened last night with the mysterious man. I wonder if he could have left the pendant for me and if so, why? I walk down the garden path then open the cast iron gate, closing it again after me and turn left towards Mr Ramsbottom's shop. I'm not going in, I haven't got any money on me anyway, I just felt like I wanted to head this way.

It's almost like an invisible force is pulling me, wiling me to come to it as I get further down the road. I walk past the shop as whatever is making me continue appears to want me to not stop yet. I notice houses and shops either side of the road now that I'm sure were never there before. It's like a village has just popped up out of nowhere. This is not like any other village I have ever been to before. There are broken and boarded up windows, graffiti everywhere and not a single person in sight. I don't like it here at all. I shiver as I walk past a deserted café, looking through the window and seeing empty tables and chairs where customers should be enjoying coffee and cakes. Next is a house that doesn't look all that old but again, seems to be deserted. I walk up to the door and try the handle, but it's locked so move on further down the road. It's very sad and depressing here. I think of the way it should be in a village of this type, people stopping to chat to each other, someone walking their dog, moms walking babies in their prams and shopkeepers laughing and joking with regulars as they make an honest living. It should be positively buzzing here but it is so far from that, and I really don't want to be here and yet here I am.

There's a small house right at the end of the road which seems to be the last building of any sort in this strange, abandoned village. As I get closer, I realize that I have seen this house before, three times to be exact. This house was depicted on the side of the cut glass goblet at my party and carved into on the lids of both mine and mom's small pendant boxes. Smoke comes from the chimney and the curtains are open. It already feels way more welcoming than the rest of the vandalised and empty village does. I knock on the traditional looking solid wooden door. There's no answer so I try again. Still, no one comes to the door. I decide to have a look through one of the front windows to see if there is any sign of life, but I can't see anyone. The fire is ablaze and there's a glass on a small table by a very comfortable looking chair which tells me that there was someone here and that they can't have been gone too long. I need to get inside and try to find out what was pulling me here, I must have some sort of connection to this quaint little house.

I come away from the window and look at the wooden front door again. There's no handle or knob on the door, just a keyhole. A crazy idea occurs to me as I take my key pendant out from underneath the top of my t-shirt, could this open the door? I pull the chain up over my head and hold out the key in my hand which is strange because although the chain was quite long when mom gave it to me, I had to undo the clasp to put it on and couldn't have taken it off without undoing it again. Taking it between my forefinger and thumb I slowly but surely put the key in the hole and turn. The door clicks open. I take the key back out of the door and put the chain with the key still attached safely back over my head with the key now dangling down to exactly where it did before I took it off.

I push the quite petite but deceivingly heavy wooden door open and step inside this curious little house. The heat from the open fire hits me straight away as the room is quite small and therefore, I am not that far away from the flames. I close the door behind me to keep the heat in and the bitter wind, which seems to have suddenly picked up, out. I was so cold walking through the desolate and depressing village as I didn't leave my house with a coat, thinking that it didn't look that chilly outside but that was in my village, it is certainly a different story here. I sit down on the firm but comfortable oxblood red leather chair to the side of the fireplace, close my eyes and just breathe for a moment, taking in the quite intoxicating smell and atmosphere a real open fire seems to give off, thinking about what a strange weekend I seem to be having when I hear a whisper. "Alex." I open my eyes instantly and look around the room. There's no one here. I stand up and look into the large golden framed mirror that hangs on the wall above the mantelpiece. I see the reflection of the wall and door behind me, but I don't see myself. I am missing, my reflection isn't here.

As I stand in front of the fire, getting warmer and warmer, the mirror starts to steam up until I can't see a reflection of anything in it at all. I keep looking at the mirror, unable somehow to look away from it, then letters start forming in the condensation as if a fingertip is writing them. I read out the words as they are written on the mirror.

THIS IS NOT YOUR TIME. YOUR FUTURE AWAITS YOU.

 I am a little puzzled to say the least by the words that are a complete riddle to me. What could 'your future awaits you' mean? I just can't make sense of the mysterious message. Of course my future awaits me, everyone's future awaits them, doesn't it? I can't do anything else but continue to my future can I? Although I can't work out what the words on the mirror mean, it is obvious to me that I'm not supposed to be here, not right now anyway so I turn around and walk back to the front door, pushing it open and stepping out into the cold air.

As I walk past the last abandoned and dilapidated shop, I breathe a sigh of relief as I know I am almost back in my own village and back in the sunshine. For the time being though I am still under a dark cloud that is like a vale of doom, and I am still freezing cold. There's Mr Ramsbottom's shop ahead sticking out like an oasis in the largest and driest of deserts. I run the rest of the way out from under the dark cloud blanket until I finally feel the warmth of the sun on my skin and know I am out of that depressing place. I stop and look back. What? Where has it gone? There's no road, no houses and shops and no dark clouds in front of me just trees, lots of them. I am

**standing in front of a forest.**

# CHAPTER 15

I couldn't have imagined walking down a street and going inside a house where there is now a forest surely. Am I going crazy? Weird things keep happening now, impossible things that I never would have thought could happen in a million years and I don't know why they are happening to me. I think maybe I just have to accept what I clearly cannot stop or change and get on with my life, there is nothing else I can do and to be honest, all of this has made me feel quite excited as well as a little scared. I think I am starting to get a little addicted to the feeling of the rush of adrenaline that has been pumping through my veins a lot lately and appears to be becoming a regular occurrence.

After a short walk I reach my house, let myself in through the front door and run straight upstairs to my bedroom. I lie down on top of my bed and stare up at the ceiling, my mind doing ten to the dozen, thoughts whirring around in there making me feel as if my head has a cyclone inside it. My brain seems to hurt now so I close my eyes and try to go to sleep, maybe it'll feel better when I wake.

I am standing on the edge of a cliff overlooking the sea. It's so beautiful and calm here in what must be a dream. An amazing feeling of contentedness flows through my whole body as I look out, completely mesmerised by the turquoise and deep blue tones of the stunning ocean before me. I turn my gaze to my right hand as I feel something in it. I am holding a small mirror. I hold the mirror up and look at my reflection. I am older. Day suddenly turns to night in the blink of an eye and now I am younger, I can feel it, I am a girl again and I'm standing in a field looking at a forest. To my right I see a large house and start walking towards it. As I approach the front door it opens automatically sensing that I am there, and I step inside. The door slams shut behind me, but I don't jump, I'm not surprised, I still feel calm and relaxed.

It's white and very shiny in here. The overpowering smell of disinfectant is making me feel a bit queasy especially as there is another smell, an undertone of something else that isn't very pleasant at all. The place looks like it's just been scrubbed, mopped and polished, it doesn't look like there's a speck of dust anywhere. This has got to be the cleanest house I've ever been in, it's almost surgically clean. Something whizzes past me as I stand not far away from the door. I don't know what it was, it went by too quickly for me to make it out and it appears to be gone now as I can't see anything in here. Something else passes me and vanishes as I look round then something else. More and more of these things rush past me and disappear into thin air and then I realise what they are, they are people.

Everything stops. All the rushing past me has ended now and it's perfectly silent in here. It feels like time itself has paused. I can't breathe. I fall to the floor fighting for air, clutching my throat desperately trying to cling onto life thinking that this is the end, that I am about to die then I wake up in my room. That was the most terrifyingly vivid dream I've ever had. I know it means something; I am sure of it. I just need to work out what that something is.

The next few days pass by quite normally. Nothing unusual or bizarre happens. I go to work, come home, have tea, watch television for a bit then go to bed, hoping I won't have another one of those dreams. I wake up early on Saturday morning, exactly a week since my birthday. My key pendant sits in the box it came in on my dressing table. I took it off that night, the night of the worst dream ever and I haven't put it back on since, I'm scared to in case wearing it is making all these strange things happen. I'll wear it again when I am ready but until then the key is staying in its box, just to be on the safe side.

I like my usual and unremarkable life. I work part time at the local animal rescue centre feeding and nurturing sick and unwanted creatures that have nowhere else to go. No animal is ever turned away, so we are always full to capacity unfortunately, which is really sad. All different species of animal are taken into the rescue such as dogs, cats and rabbits plus the more exotic kind like lizards, snakes and even a bird that's apparently native to an island off New Zealand that I've never heard of, I have no idea what it is doing in England. I do a few half days at the rescue centre during the week and a full day on a Saturday which is the busiest day there. I can never wait to go to work. I absolutely love my job and I know not everyone is able to say that, so I think myself lucky work wise. I have a wash, get dressed, tie my hair up in a high ponytail and then make my way downstairs to fill up on toast with butter and strawberry jam for breakfast.

Although I am thoroughly looking forward to going to the centre today to look after the animals, I can't stop thinking about everything that's happened in the last week, especially the man I briefly met at my party, the one with eyes like infinity pools that I could get lost in forever. I feel like I've had that thought before and felt like this before but how could I have when we only met last week? Well, I say met, we didn't really meet, properly that is as we didn't even speak but I felt that we had a connection, the man and I and I must find him, I have to know who he is.

I grab my umbrella as I am about to leave the house as I hear heavy raindrops on the front window which are getting louder and louder. I like the sound of the rain, it's a comforting sound. I would rather listen to it inside than having to walk outside in it, but I have got to brave the weather and start the journey to work. Oh well, here we go I think to myself as I open the front door and close it behind me, stepping out into the pouring rain. It's not too bad actually, walking through what was a torrential down pour moments ago but is now more of a steady flow of smaller droplets underneath my bright pink umbrella which I bought a few weeks ago because I absolutely loved the colour. No one will miss me under this! I splash through puddle after puddle each seeming deeper than the last as I continue my soggy journey. I wonder if there will be any new animals brought into the centre today. Maybe a tarantula or an iguana, a chinchilla would be nicer though.

"Hi Helen" I say when I see my boss. I say boss but Helen is more like a colleague and a friend than a boss. "Morning chick" Helen says in her usual bright and cheery tone. I put my bag in my locker in the staff room, make myself a cup of coffee then step back out into the corridor and head towards the domestic pet area of the rescue centre. It really is a huge place with acres of land outside for all sorts of different animals to explore to their hearts content. The animals have a great life here, far better usually than the life they would have had before they came here. When I enter section one, I hear lots of barking, a bit of growling and some whining from the array of dogs of all shapes and sizes here. There are Staffordshire Bull Terrier's, Boxers, German Shepherds and even a tiny miniature wired haired Dachshund all safely in their own kennels.

I love dogs and I could quite easily take the Dachshund home with me, but I don't think I would have enough time to care for that kind of animal with most of my time taken up going to university and coming here to work. I can't expect mom to look after a dog for me and besides she is more of a cat person as am I really. I would take a cat home. I just haven't found the right one yet.

I don't know why I don't just quit university and work here full time. I love my job so much and can't really see myself doing anything else for work. I am studying to be become a nurse. I have nearly finished the course, but I am not at all sure that I want to do what I've trained for over the last few years. This is my life, the animals, I love them all no matter how big or small, fluffy or smooth they are, to me each creature is a perfect creation of nature.

As I leave section one and enter section two (which is my favourite) I hear lots of meowing. There are cats of all different breeds and colours, but the majority are the black and white non pedigree kind. As I come to the end of the first row of cats, I see a tiny kitten huddled at the back of the cage. As soon the kitten sees me it comes to the front of the cage and starts purring. The kitten's fluffy coat is a blue/grey colour, and it has peculiar but gorgeous eyes, one orange and one green. This cute little kitten seems so familiar to me like lots of other things have done recently. Maybe it's just that he seems to have taken a liking to me and there is no other reason for me to think that I might already know this little feline ball of fur. I open the cage and instantly the kitten jumps into my arms and curls up, purring and looking at me with those big beautiful, odd eyes. "I'm going to call you Henry" I say, deciding the kitten is a boy. "I'm taking you home at the end of the day. You are going to come and live with me."

# CHAPTER 16

It's been a few weeks since I brought Henry into our family home. He has settled in so well and everyone loves him, you couldn't not, he's the sweetest little thing. Henry follows me everywhere. He even sleeps on my bed, it's like he can't bear to be away from me. Either that or he's trying to protect me, like a guard dog would. He's the best friend I never knew I needed, and I cannot imagine my life without my little blue ball of fluff. Henry is never happy on the days I go off to university or work, but I try and hurry back to be with him again. He runs straight up to the front door when he hears my key in it, it really is like I've got a dog and not a cat.

Today is a free day for me so I decide to go to the park with Henry tagging along, keeping me company. He just walks by the side of me on the way, as close to my feet as he can without getting accidentally kicked and stays close by when we get into the park. I didn't think previously that cats behaved like Henry does. I thought cats were quite independent and could take or leave human beings really but not my cat, he's special. Henry and I walk past the swings and slide and on to the large duck pond. I thought that maybe Henry would try to chase the ducks and geese like I'm sure most cats would, but he just sits by my feet when I stop beside the pond throwing oats and seeds out into the water to feed the birds.

Henry and I start walking around to the other side of the pond then, up ahead I spot a tunnel made entirely of trees. I can't resist walking through the tunnel made completely by nature and of course Henry comes too, loyal as ever. When we come to the end of the tunnel of trees there is a path that forks into two. I don't remember ever seeing this path here in the park before. Come to think of it I don't recall the tunnel made of trees either. I stand and stare in one direction which the path forks off to and then the other, puzzled as to why I have not previously noticed it as I have walked around this pond many times in the past. One path bends and appears to continue around the duck pond, and I presume back to where we started, the other ascends up a steep hill. I am intrigued to find out where the mysterious uphill path leads and far too curious a person not to climb this one, so I take the plunge and step forward. As soon as I do so the path starts to crack and then break up until it is very uneven looking and quite dangerous to walk on as I could easily trip and fall over. Trying my utmost to be careful and not lose my footing on the now very rough terrain I determinedly carry on regardless without the slightest thought of turning back. I must find out what is over the other side of this hill, I can't explain why but the feeling gets stronger and stronger the further I get towards the top. When I get to the top of the hill, Henry still beside me, I step onto grass. I am in a field now and not in my local park anymore.

There's a wooden shack up ahead with a sign on the roof that's lit up which reads 'Megan's place' in quite retro looking letters. It looks so out of place, like it should be on the bank of a swamp in the deep south of Mississippi not in England. Assuming I am still in England of course. I step forward towards the shack and glance back noticing that Henry has stopped and is not right beside me anymore. He looks at me from the top of the hill with those unusual and knowing eyes like he is not just a cat, like he has a higher intelligence as well as emotion, and stays put as if he is refusing to go any further. "Ok Henry you stay there, I'm just going to have a look in there" I say pointing at the small, dilapidated shack. I know Henry won't go anywhere and will wait for me, so I continue to 'Megan's place'.

I push the wooden door open easily and to my surprise I am about to step into a place that looks nothing like how I thought it would from the outside. There's a very grand looking staircase cascading down to the left of me, a slope up to an elegant bar to my right and the most glamorous and enormous ballroom straight ahead down two beautiful marble steps. I am in complete shock while I look around trying to take in the amazing interior of what I thought was a small and run-down old shack. The chandeliers that hang down from the extremely high ceiling sparkle so brilliantly and the finger food being offered on shiny silver trays look almost too good to eat. Everyone here looks perfect. The ladies are dressed in ball gowns and the men are reminiscent of prince charming from the most intriguing of fairy tales in dapper suits with cravats, waistcoats and tails. I realise that I am completely underdressed and feel very out of place then look down and see that I am wearing my long blue dress I wore for my birthday party weeks ago. I don't know how that happened. I had scruffy jeans and a t-shirt on before I got here. Well at least I look the part now and can probably blend in quite well with the rest of the people here.

I must find out what this place is all about. I need to know what it is doing in the middle of a gigantic field that should have been the other side of the park and how the hell it is so big in here when it looks so much smaller on the outside. I recognise the name Megan but I'm not sure why. Maybe somebody with that name was in one of my dreams, I don't know though, it feels more like a memory than a dream, the same as all my dreams do. I think back to the last time I wore this dress and what happened that night. Maybe just maybe there might be a sliver of a chance that he'll be here, the man I cannot get out of my head that I met on my twenty first birthday.

I head up the polished slope towards the bar so I can order a drink as I am thirsty after all the walking I did before getting here. I approach the bar and without looking up the lady standing behind it says, "what can I get you Alex?" What? How does she know my name? I don't say anything. I guess I am stunned that a stranger somehow knows who I am. The lady looks up at me and asks again "what can I get you?" "Um, um, just a lemonade please" I manage to get out, stuttering a little. "Coming right up" the lady says then almost instantly puts a glass of clear fizzy liquid down on the bar in front of me. I lift the glass up and put it to my lips taking a sip of the cold refreshing lemony drink. I put the glass back down and say thank you. "That'll be £1.80 please" the bar lady says. I start to panic, realizing that I haven't got as much as a penny on me. I only left the house with small bags of food for the ducks and geese in the park. "Only joking Lex, it's on the house" the bar lady says. As I look up at her she winks and then walks to the other end of the bar to serve someone else.

Not many people call me Lex. Only people who know me really well call me that, usually just my sister come to think of it. I don't even know how she knows my name at all let alone the shortened version only certain people use as a nickname. I'm not going to get any answers to the questions present in my head right now so decide to take my drink and explore this magnificent space more starting with the very grand looking ballroom.

There's a small staircase directly in front of me that leads down onto the floor of the ballroom so, conveniently I don't have to go all the way back down the slope to get to it. I am totally overwhelmed by the size of the room. It must be as big if not bigger than a football pitch with exquisite crystal chandeliers dangling down making the stunning polished glittery floor sparkle like a clear night sky full of bright stars. I imagine myself dancing around the floor with my very own prince charming or even just a handsome stranger and cast my mind back to the night of my birthday once again. I wish he was here, that stranger that has somehow managed to steal my heart with a glance and a touch of the hand. Is this what love at first sight is? I need to see him again. The feeling hasn't left me since we met. I've never seen such piercing blue eyes on anyone else. Or have I. I don't know, maybe someone in another of my dreams perhaps. Again, I feel like it's more of a memory, like a flashback, I think. Something seems to be coming back to me now anyway, something that has actually happened. I am sure of it. Have I met my mystery man before? Have I looked into those eyes previously, the ones that remind me of staring at a tranquil ocean on a beautiful summer day?

I feel a hand on my shoulder. I turn around and he's standing there. "May I have this dance?" the man I have been daydreaming about asks. He's here. It is him; I can't believe it! I just look at him, smile timidly and take his hand as he leads me to the centre of the dance floor. A band strikes up instantly and starts to play a lovely romantic piece of music as I am whisked around without a care in the world in this perfect moment. I didn't know I could dance like this and yet here I am doing it, knowing all the steps, seeming to instinctively put one foot forward then one to the left then back naturally in what I think is a waltz. I feel free and deliriously happy as I spin round and round getting slightly dizzy but totally loving every second all the same. Faster and faster we go until I realise, I am not being held anymore. I stop and steady myself looking around desperately for my handsome dance partner. He's gone. Everyone has gone. I am completely alone.

I haven't been up the elaborate staircase yet that is now to my right from where I am standing. I walk over to the staircase and begin climbing up the shiny marble steps. I need to find out what's going on in this curious place. I notice there are pictures on the walls on the way up the staircase. There are pictures of houses, of cliffs and of beaches. There's even a church that looks extremely familiar and a field with a forest beyond it that I swear I have been to before. Every picture I look at seems to mean something to me and I think of my dreams. I have dreamt about these buildings and places but why are they documented as framed watercolours hanging on a massive wall above this staircase? I push forward, onwards and upwards trying not to look at any more dreamlike pictures, step by step, higher and higher until I finally get to the top.

The floor is whitewashed wooden boards up here. The walls are painted pale pink and pretty curtains with a teddy bear print on them hang either side of a small window. The room itself, which must be directly above the grand ballroom, is much smaller than I had expected it to be. This can't be it surely, there must be more rooms up here. There aren't any doors, and the stairs go straight into this room so if there are any more, I don't know how they can be reached. As I step further into the room, I see a cot in an alcove over in the corner. I walk over to the cot to see if there's a baby inside it sleeping silently only to find it empty except for a yellow knitted blanket. I pick up the blanket and smell it without having a clue why. It smells so good. I can't really describe it, but it smells like home, not the home I live in now but a different sort, just home. A strange feeling begins to wash over me and the smell changes. I drop the blanket and I sit down on the floor thinking I may faint if I continue to stand. I put my head in my hands and rub my temples with my thumbs. My head hurts. It's probably the shock of all this, this place, dancing with my prince charming and the dream like pictures. Smelling that blanket didn't help. I don't know why I did it, it just made sense at the time but now I think maybe it wasn't such a good idea as the headache that is now getting worse might have been caused by the scent. I feel really faint now and the room is spinning. Everything is going black...

Where am I? I'm lying on cold ground looking up at very tall trees. I hear a meow and slowly sit up. It looks like I am close to the edge of a forest. Henry is sitting right in front of me purring and looking me straight in the eye. I'm so glad he is here with me. I pull myself up to my feet, ouch my head really hurts. I want to sit back down again, to lie on the ground until the pain stops but I don't. I feel like there's no time to lose, like I need to move. I slowly walk with Henry at my side once more towards an apparent open space where the trees seem to end. My head is still pounding but with every step I take it eases slightly until, by the time I step onto the green grass of a huge field, the pain is completely gone, and I feel alright again.

I look around in every direction. There is only grass as far as the eye can see, apart from the trees behind me. I decide to turn left as that way is as good as any I guess and follow the edge of the forest instead of walking forward across the field. Nothing really changes as I walk past tree after tree, each looking the same as the last. I feel as if I am going round in circles. I look out across the field but there's nothing different there either, everything is just the same as it was when I started walking. I look up at the clouds for a few moments then notice something very odd. They're not moving. The clouds are perfectly still. Clouds always move, even when there seems to be no breeze at all, it is part of nature, they do not just stand still. I turn my attention back to the forest and something occurs to me; maybe I am going round in circles. Maybe I'm walking and not really getting anywhere at all.

I pick up a small rock and scratch the closest tree with it to make a mark. Testing my theory, I continue to walk thinking that if I am going in a circle, eventually I will come back to this tree. After about half an hour I wonder if I was correct at all about not getting anywhere different then come across the tree with the mark scratched into the bark. Well, I thought it was the mark that I had made but I thought I had only scratched a line into the trunk of the tree, this looks more like an arrow. It's pointing upwards. Does it mean straight ahead or indeed straight up the tree? I am good at climbing, but this is the tallest tree I have ever seen, and I am not sure I fancy going up it. Do I give it a try to see what is up there, if anything, or do I take the, perhaps, safer option of heading into the forest? I think the climb might be the way I should go; it feels like something is telling me to go for it. Besides, I don't know what's in the forest, it looks quite dark and does seem a little creepy.

The first few branches are quite low so it's easy to start the climb up this extremely tall tree. Henry stays on the first branch looking up at me as if he's willing me to continue but won't follow me. I can do this. I reach up to the next branch then the next, climbing higher and higher up the tree. I tell myself to not look down but of course I can't help it and I do then instantly wish I hadn't at such a dizzying height. I panic, close my eyes and start breathing far too quickly. I can't move, like I'm glued to the spot, and I feel like I might just pass out when I hear a strange sound that snaps me out of my apparent acrophobia that I seem to have suddenly acquired. "Squawk" there's that sound again. It's the sort of sound a bird makes but not like any bird I have heard before, it's so loud and has a low tone then higher pitched one at the end. My breathing starts to slow down as I wonder about the creature making the unusual sound. I open my eyes and look up to see a brightly coloured sort of bird like creature perched high up on one of the branches of this ridiculously tall tree.

I start climbing again, up and up getting closer to the curious squawk that the strange looking creature is making. At last, I reach up for what must be the last branch and pull myself up, pushing with my feet on a lower one. This isn't another branch but a ledge I have managed to haul my body onto, collapsing in a heap from the exhaustion of the massive and intense climb. I sit up and look around realising quickly that I am not just on a ledge and that there is a little wooden house attached at the end of this rather large platform. I always wanted a tree house when I was a child but never imagined I would end up in front of one on top of a tree that must be around three hundred feet tall. I catch my breath as I try and take in how high up I really am. The air is thinner up here and it is harder to breathe now. I have no idea why I decided to climb up to the top of the tree instead of just walking in another direction on the ground, but I certainly intend to find out.

I stand up and walk towards the tree house. There isn't a door to open, just a space where a door could be so slowly, I step inside. It's in here now, the strange bird like creature. It's blue, green, red and golden feathers are so brightly coloured, it is prettier than the very proudest of peacocks. "Squawk" the creature makes that sound again and looks straight at me, right into my eyes as if it knows me. "Hello to you too" I answer without thinking of how bizarre this scenario would look to anyone else. I don't know how I knew what the creature said but I know it said hello to me, I understand the language and I don't just hear a squawk anymore.

"My name is Exodus, and I am the last of my kind, the very last one of the beesha's." "What's a beesha?" I ask still surprised that I can understand what the vividly coloured creature is saying to me. "Why a bird of course, at the moment anyway but just lately a cat most of the time." "What, what do you mean a cat?" I ask, thinking how on earth a bird can also be a cat. "You seem to like calling me Henry" answers the bird. "Henry?" I look deep into the strange bird's eyes, one orange, one green and sudden, overwhelming realisation hits me like I've been punched in the stomach, it is him, it's my cat Henry.

"I don't understand. How are you a bird, one that I have never heard of and a cat?" I ask, now kneeling on the floor of the small tree house. "I am not from your time Alex. I am from the future when all creatures on earth are almost extinct. You are our only chance of survival. Only you can save everything, every human, every animal and every plant, all life." Exodus, or Henry as I usually know him explains that he had to come to the past, my present, in the form of a domestic pet, something he knew that I would like, a cat, a very cute one that I wouldn't be able to resist taking home with me so he could be close to me, help me by guiding me in my quest to save the planet. How am I going to save the world? Why me, why not someone else? I don't get it. "I'm sorry I couldn't come to you in my natural form, but I guess you wouldn't have invited a Beesha bird to come and live with you and your family" Exodus says. Of course I wouldn't. He is obviously right. I totally understand why he did it, transformed into a cat that is, but it is blowing my mind that he can do it. "Will you be there as Henry when I get down from here?" I ask tentatively. "We're not going down" Exodus says and walks out of the tree house and onto the ledge which is now much bigger than it was before. I follow him out into the open air and watch as he appears to grow before my eyes. Exodus's wings expand, his chest puffs out and all the other colours seem to fade away until he is entirely golden, sparkling in the sunlight. I am aghast at Exodus in all his wonderful glory. I have never seen anything so magnificent in my life. My little Henry is now quite an extraordinary sight to behold.

"Jump on. We haven't got much time" Exodus says. "What do you mean?" I ask him. "Jump on my back, come on we need to go" he says, more desperately this time. I don't even ask where to and, not wishing to waste another second as this amazing creature seems to be getting more and more perplexed the longer I take to move, I climb onto his huge back. "Hold on" Exodus says and starts flapping his wings which must each be at least two metres long. He starts running and in no time we're off the ledge, away from the tree house and gliding through the sky.

This is the most amazing feeling, there must be absolutely nothing like it in the whole world. I feel safe up here, flying through the sky on a huge gold bird, safe and serene like nothing else matters but this moment, right here, right now. We fly over trees then field after field on this epic journey to goodness only knows where. I am just thoroughly enjoying this unusual flight and I am not sure I care that much about where we're headed. I love this feeling, gliding through the sky on the back of my best friend in the world. I lie down on soft feathers that feel like a cross between silk and velvet and close my eyes, feeling so calm and relaxed that I could go to sleep.

"Alex, we're almost here" Exodus exclaims and wakes me from a dream I have never had before. I dreamt of a normal life. A life with a man I was in love with. I never saw his face in my dream, but I know he was the love of my life, I can still feel it. We land on water, the sea I presume. "You need to go on your own now" Exodus says looking round at me. I slide off his back as he starts shrinking back down to eventually be the size he was when we were inside the tree house, about the size of a large duck I suppose but with longer legs. "Go where?" I ask, confused to say the least. Exodus looks down at the gentle waves then looks back up at me smiling through his beautiful eyes and flies off. "Go where?" I shout after him but it's no good, he's already gone, disappearing quickly into the blue.

I tread water in the cool turquoise ocean for a few moments then abruptly start being pulled down towards the seabed. It's not someone pulling me down but some sort of force. I am not holding my breath, I can breathe underwater, and I don't feel the need to panic at all, I feel calm in fact. I am calm, I am strong and determined. Whatever it is that has been pulling me stops and instead I start swimming down towards the invisible force that is now willing me to it. I see a light ahead. I swim closer to it and pass through into the unknown.

# CHAPTER 17

How can I be here? I never expected this. I thought that maybe I had died and was swimming towards heaven's door or it was some kind of crazy dream, and I would wake up back in my bed again, anything else than where I am. It's warm in here as it always was. I am standing inside the veranda at granddads house. Granddad died when I was twelve and the house was sold to people I don't know so how and why am I here? I open the glass door and see two more doors, one to the toilet on my left and one to the kitchen on my right. I open the kitchen door and the smell hits me. Apple pie! It can't be can it. "Alexandra come on in, I've been expecting you." "Granddad, is that really you?" I rub my eyes not quite believing who I am seeing. It really is my granddad standing here right in front of me. "I know it's hard to believe but you have gone back to the past, back again I mean" granddad says "again?" I ask, wondering what he means by that. "You've been here before Alex, in the past here with me a long time ago when you were a child. You didn't have to go too far back that time. You've had to go back much further this time though" Granddad says and looks at me with his kind eyes.

I try to make sense of what granddad is saying to me while still reeling from the fact that I am here with him. It's all so weird, I don't even know what to do, what to think or feel right now. "Sit down Alex" granddad says in the soft, soothing voice I remember from my childhood. I sit on the comfy old leather sofa that is the same as it was all those years ago, well-worn but well loved. I feel the warmth of granddad's hands as he takes mine in his and starts explaining everything to me. "You had to start again Alex. Your life wasn't exactly heading in the direction it should have been." "What do you mean? What did I do wrong?" I ask granddad feeling more confused than ever. "You didn't do anything wrong" he continues, "but you made some decisions that would have impacted the future in a very negative way unfortunately. I can't tell you what those decisions were or when they happened, all I can say is that you need to change something that you did before by the time you get to thirty." "Why thirty?" I ask an animated granddad. "I can't tell you that either I'm afraid, if I tell you too much it could change things in a different way from the way things should happen. It must happen naturally. It must be totally your decision made with the help of your intuition, your gift" granddad smiles and lets me speak now. "Ok so let me get this straight, I need to go back to my normal life in the present and change something within the next nine years, but I don't know exactly when, where or what that something is." "Yes" is granddads reply. I sigh and then take a very deep breath and start rubbing my temples. "Here take one of these, it'll help" granddad says holding a small bag of teacakes which seem to have appeared out of nowhere. I am not sure how eating one of these will help with my situation right now, but I pick one and put it in my mouth regardless, they are my favourite sweets after all. It tastes amazing and somehow makes me feel light and drowsy like I can I hardly keep my eyes open.

I open my eyes and stare at the ceiling. I'm in my bedroom lying in my lovely cosy bed. I sit up and stretch. That was the most amazingly vivid dream I have ever had, seeming even more real than any of my previous ones. What is that taste in my mouth? It tastes like toffee but there's something else...coconut. It tastes like I have just eaten a teacake sweet. Was it a dream? Surely a dream can't make you taste something that you dreamt you were eating while you were fast asleep.

Henry jumps up onto my bed and meows. He gives that

familiar knowing look like he's more than just a cat, like he is wiser, more intelligent and more of a friend than simply a pet. "Oh, Henry was it real?" I ask him as he makes himself comfortable on my lap. He looks up at me, meows again and I swear he winks with his orange eye. I squeeze my eyes shut tightly, shake my head then open my eyes again not quite believing what I just saw my cat do. Henry is now at the door looking back at me. I think he wants me to follow him. Where is he going to take me and is this going to be another adventure that is real and actually happens but leads me to believe it was all merely a dream? I follow Henry into the kitchen where he stands by the cupboard. He knows his food is kept in there and just looks at me and meows. "Oh, you just want your breakfast" I say laughing and shaking my head. Henry is just hungry, and I guess I did just have a dream last night.

# CHAPTER 18

**2015**

Everything has been quite normal for me since I was twenty-one. I finished my degree in nursing and just about scraped through with a pass (which was probably because I decided a while ago that nursing really wasn't for me). Working with animals is all I have ever really wanted to do so I am now working full time at the rescue centre. I haven't seen the mysterious handsome man again in my dreams although I still think about him. I have never really been able to get him fully out of my head even though I know I should. I have met someone else now anyway, a vet called Tom who works at the local surgery. We've been dating for around six months now and the relationship is getting serious. Tom has asked me to move into his very modern and extremely tidy flat which might prove to be a little taxing for me if I do move in with him as I am certainly not the tidiest person in the world and I have a thing for more traditional styles when it comes to interior design. I do like spending time at Tom's but have always imagined living in a quaint little cottage in the countryside not a penthouse apartment overlooking the city. I guess I don't really have that much of a choice where we live as Tom is the breadwinner and he already has a mortgage on his flat whereas I still live with my mom and sister.

My dreams are still as vivid and recurring, but I know that dreams are all they ever were, nothing more than that. I love Tom, I do, it's just that in my heart of hearts I always thought I would feel more than I do, be more madly and passionately in love with the person I ended up with. Tom is totally in love with me, I am pretty sure of that and that is enough for me right now. I am going to do it, I have made up my mind, I am going to say yes to Tom and move in with him. I can't stay at home forever and the thought of living together is quite exciting.

I ring the Chinese restaurant that is a few roads away from home to book a table for tonight. It's going to be so romantic. We'll have wine and delicious food then I'll tell Tom that I will move in with him and he'll be so happy, I can just picture it. I will be happy too; I am happy in general but there is just this feeling that never really goes away. I can't really explain it other than saying it's like an itch that needs ultimately to be scratched and it irritates me a tiny bit more every day.

There's a knock at the door. It's 7.30pm. Tom is here as he had said he would be, absolutely on time to the minute. He is so reliable. I always know he will be on time, and he won't let me down. I really like that about him. I open the door and there he stands, my soon to be cohabiting partner dressed very smartly in crisp white shirt and dark well pressed trousers, holding out a beautiful big bunch of red roses. Tom knows roses are my favourite flowers so every time we go out on a date, he brings me a massive bunch. "Come in for a minute while I put the flowers in some water" I say and hurry to the kitchen conscious of the time. The table is booked for 7.45pm and Tom hates being late for anything, even if it is only a few minutes. I rush back to the front door after digging out mom's one and only vase from the kitchen cupboard, filling it with water and dropping the roses into it in a very haphazard manner. "You will have to sort those out later, they need to be cut diagonally on the ends and arranged properly" Tom announces. "Will do" I reply as we make our way out to Tom's car.

It's a brand new bright white four by four with luxurious leather seats and all the bells and whistles you can imagine in a car as expensive as this one must have been. Tom makes quite a lot of money as a vet, but he doesn't really need to work as his dad is a count who lives in an actual castle! Not that that bothers me at all, I would be happy if his dad worked as a dustbin man as long as he was a nice person. He is a nice person as well as being extremely rich and having a title which I am relieved about as I thought that maybe stereotypically, he may be close minded and look down on people like me who are more working class. Tom lost his mother when he was little, and he hardly remembers her unlike me with my dad. I still really miss him. I wish he would come to me in my dreams like granddad does. I wonder why it is always granddad that graces me with his presence in my slumber. Why is he significant in my dreams, if in fact he is at all? Maybe I need some sort of therapy. Perhaps I have never actually come to terms with my granddad's death, and I can't move on or past it in some way. I'll see what Tom thinks about it, we should probably talk about it later.

I do like this car, it's really comfortable and I can see everything around me outside as the seats are so high up. I would love to have a go at driving it, but Tom won't let me. He says it's too big, too much car for me to handle and that he is just trying to protect me from a possible accident. I know he only has my best interests at heart, but I wish he wouldn't wrap me up in cotton wool so much. I feel like Tom sees me as a china doll sometimes that could be broken very easily.

We pull up outside the restaurant about five minutes after we left my house and get out of the brilliant white car. I hope we get our table. It's the booth in the corner that is so cosy and romantic with velvet cushions on the seats for comfort. Tom holds the door open, and I step inside the elaborately decorated Chinese restaurant complete with a giant dragon made entirely of paper suspended from the ceiling with thin wires that you can only see if you look very carefully. Tom gives his name to the waiter who immediately leads us over to the booth I was hoping for. We sit down and Tom orders a bottle of the most expensive white wine on the menu. I would prefer a glass or two of pink fizzy sweet wine but as Tom is paying, I don't say anything. I can drink white wine but it's not my favourite.

"So" Tom begins, "why are we here tonight?" "Well," I say looking right into his eyes, "I wanted to talk to you about something." "Oh yes and what might that something be?" Tom asks me, smiling, his perfectly white teeth almost glowing in the dim light of ultra-low wattage bulbs in pretty lamps dotted about on walls and tea light candles on tabletops. Tom is just about as perfect boyfriend material as a man could possibly be and even though I have a niggling feeling that I am not one hundred percent sure about how I feel I can put that aside for a predictable and safe life with someone who loves me as much as he obviously does.

"Yes!" I announce. "Yes?" Tom says with a puzzled look on his face. "Yes, I'll move in with you" I say. Tom grins and takes my hands in his. "That's brilliant news Alex! I'm so glad you made the right decision. Let's tell your mom tomorrow and get it sorted in the next few days" Tom says excitedly. I have to say, I am a little shocked, I didn't realise it would all happen so soon. I'm not sure I am ready. I thought I would be at home for a few more weeks at least not just a few days. I say nothing to Tom and instead just smile, going along with what he has suggested then picking up the menu.

# CHAPTER 19

It's Saturday and today is moving out of the family home and into Tom's flat day. It's a weird feeling, I mean I have lived in the same house for the last twenty-five years and a big part of me doesn't really want to leave. I tell myself that I need to grow up and get on with it in a matter-of-fact way. I have got to move out of home sometime anyway so why not now and why not with a man who can offer me so much. Yes, I am doing this, I really am. I swallow my emotions that are just bubbling under the surface and get on with the job of packing the last few things from my bedroom including my silver key pendant still on the chain that mom gave me into one of the cardboard boxes then sealing it with brown parcel tape. I have been really organized (which is unusual for me) and written on the boxes what is in each of them with black marker pen. This one simply says 'odds and ends' as I didn't know what else to put and even if I am going to keep all the items I have put into it. The key pendant comes under the category of 'odds and ends' because I haven't worn it for years. I haven't taken it out of the box in ages and still have no idea who gave it to me as a present for my twenty-first birthday.

I will decide what to do with all this stuff later when I unpack it in my new home. I am panicking a little about living in such a clean and tidy place as I am not the world's most tidy person and actually prefer a bit of clutter and disorganisation. Tom is so opposite; I am not sure how I am going to handle living together full time. I guess I will just have to learn to change a bit, to fit around the way Tom lives. I think I can learn how to be a more organised and tidier person. I'm going to have to try my best to change from the way I am (a bit messy and scatty) as Tom gets pretty stressed out if things aren't in the right place or the place he has put them in anyway. I am sure that things will work themselves out eventually even if I am the one who has to bend to fit.

I pick up a box, carry it downstairs and then take it outside to the removal van that is parked half on the pavement in front of the wonderful little house that I am leaving behind very soon. I don't think a van is entirely necessary as I don't have that much stuff, it would have fitted into Tom's car, but he insisted on having removal men to help me as it would all just be easier. That's it. All my worldly belongings are in the back of this van. I give Beth then mom a hug and wipe the tears from my eyes while I climb into the passenger seat of this large high sided vehicle.

The town I am moving to is not too far away in distance, but it is a world away from the pretty little village I am used to with rolling countryside all around it. At least I can go back and visit whenever I like which I think will be quite often, I miss my family so much already. I miss Henry too. I can't bring him with me because pets aren't allowed in the apartment block where Tom lives so we agreed Henry would have to stay with mom and Beth. It's going to be very strange without my best friend following me around and jumping on my bed first thing in the morning purring so loudly that he wakes me up. Tears well in my eyes again and I feel like telling the driver to turn around, to go back, that I can't do it, but I don't and sit slumped against the window instead, quietly sobbing.

I put the first box down onto the sumptuous cream carpet of this extremely modern and perfectly organized apartment on the top floor of a very tall building and walk across the living room toward the floor-to-ceiling windows. I look out over the city at all the roof tops of other buildings. It's not quite the view I am used to seeing but it is breath-taking in a different way all the same. This is what I will see every day when I wake up from now on and I think I can live with that, just about.

Tom won't be back from work until 6pm so I have all day to unpack and find brand new places for all my worldly goods. The removal man brings up the last of the boxes and places it in the hallway along with the others. I thank him, hand over a twenty-pound note as a tip as instructed to do so by Tom and close the front door. Ok that's it, I'm in and I have done it. I have moved from my family, my cat and my beloved little village to the big city.

After getting all my clothes, books, my old teddy bear and everything from my dressing table including the photo of mom, dad, Beth and me out of boxes and finding places for them in the flat I put my feet up and turn on the TV. I get up off the huge immaculate cream leather corner sofa that I was slightly worried about sitting on without a throw over it and go to the kitchen to see if there is any interesting looking food in the fridge. I open the massive American style fridge to find that all the food inside looks far too healthy and not very appetizing to me at all. Well, that's disappointing. I guess I'll just grab an apple and see if there's anything that I would be tempted to eat in any of the cupboards, there are plenty of them to look in after all. Cupboard after cupboard I open briefly then close again as I can't find anything I fancy then in the last one I see something that takes me right back to my childhood. How did Tom know about my all-time favourite sweets? I am pretty sure I've never mentioned loving them to him. I didn't think Tom would be that interested in confectionary, he doesn't eat sweets. I take the small bag of sugary delights and go back into the living room settling back down in front of the TV. I undo the knot in the top of the small plastic bag and take out a teacake, studying it for just a moment before popping it into my mouth and smiling to myself. If heaven was simply a taste, then this is what it would taste like to me.

I wake up with a start. Tom is sitting on the sofa next to me with his hand on my leg. The room is dark apart from the light from the TV. "What time is it?" I ask Tom, sitting up and stretching. "I'm back later than I wanted to be. It's 10 o'clock" Tom says looking at his watch. I must have fallen asleep. I've been asleep for hours then. I must have been really tired. I question why Tom is back this late as he said he'd be back from work by 6pm. He says he had forgotten he had a meeting with his boss to discuss becoming a partner at the practice. I can't complain really, it's a good thing and I know it is what Tom wants but I wish he had let me know when he realised he was going to be late, a text or phone call would have woken me up earlier.

It's 9am and I am alone again. Tom has an emergency with a cow on a farm on the outskirts of town. I am in awe of his dedication to the animals. That's kind of why I fell for him in the first place. It's really warm already, mid-June and the temperature has been hitting 30 degrees in certain parts of the country for the last few weeks. I decide to put my swimsuit on with a thin maxi dress over the top, grab a towel and then check out the roof top pool. Yesterday I was a little down, sad about leaving home and lonely in the flat on my own. I didn't feel like doing anything but moping around then but today is a brand-new day and I am sure a swim will do me good.

Wow! It's amazing up here! The pool is beautiful and so inviting in this lovely sunshine. The crystal-clear water shimmers gloriously and I can't wait to dive in. There's even a bar at the side, a swim up one like you might find abroad at one of those snazzy five-star hotels. As I walk towards the pool a man calls out to me, "Hi Alex." How does he know my name? I have never met this man before. Tom must have told him about me and described me then said that I would be moving in. I am the only other person on the roof top right now, so I suppose it was an educated guess. "Hi" I say back to the man before slipping off my dress, draping it, along with my bright pink towel, over a sun lounger and then diving into the deep end of the pool. Oh, it feels so good gliding through the lovely warm water. I could get used to this.

I must have been swimming underwater for around thirty seconds when I head up to the surface. I draw my hands up over my face and the top of my head to get the majority of the water off myself and open my eyes. What? What is this? It can't be! Everything is different. The bar has gone, and I am no longer in a pool. It's dark. Day has turned into night, and I think that I am in the middle of an ocean. I am getting cold, and I'm scared now. "Squawk" I hear a familiar sound, one from my dreams and turn around. "Exodus" I say remembering the brightly coloured bird from last night when I was asleep. "Squawk" he makes the sound again and then starts to grow and change. Golden feathers sparkle and shine in the moonlight as the bird spreads his huge wings. "Get on" he says not squawking anymore and speaking proper words. I can understand him. I might as well do as Exodus says having clearly no other plausible way to get out of the water so climb onto his back trying not to pull at his glorious feathers too much. I hold on as tightly as I can around his thick neck which he appears to hardly feel, and my beautiful mode of transport and apparent rescuer takes flight.

We soar above the ocean, Exodus and I gliding through the clear night sky, bright stars above us giving off a little light as well as the perfectly full moon. It's an extraordinary sight looking down at the gentle waves shimmering like translucent yet silvery mother of pearl, not another soul in sight. I feel like I am the only person in the world right now as a wonderful calmness hits then washes over and through me like a spot of paint from a brush gently touching clear still water, the colour expanding, slowly mixing and diluting, the water accepting the paint and welcoming it with flowing open arms.

I snap out of my almost trance like state when a thought occurs to me. "Where are we going?" I shout to Exodus but I'm not sure I am happy with his response, "you will see" is all he says. What does that even mean? It wasn't much of an answer and certainly not what I was hoping to hear but I don't say anything else on this bizarre journey to goodness knows where, feeling like the huge golden bird I am lying on isn't going to tell me anything more.

Ahead I see hills and trees. I look down and the water, now shallow, seems to be evaporating before my very eyes until there is no longer an ocean below us but streets and houses. We land with a thud. I am on the roof of a building. I look across and down the road. I recognise it. I know where I am. The pet shop is opposite so that means Exodus and I are standing on top of the Chinese restaurant that Tom and I ate in a few nights ago. "Goodbye Alex" Exodus says looking deeply into my eyes, almost searching for something in me then without warning, flies off, shrinking and changing colour to include red, green and blue as he makes his way into the distance.

Well, I guess this is where I am meant to be then. Now I need to get down from the roof and inside the restaurant. It looks like the only way is to slide down the roof and onto the guttering. I'll then have to drop down onto the small balcony outside the window of the flat on the first floor of the building. After that I'm not sure but here goes. Down the tiles I slide then hit the guttering with the soles of my boots I now appear to be wearing. I am also fully clothed in jeans and a t-shirt. I have no idea how that happened, but I am glad I'm not in my swimsuit anymore. I hold on to the guttering hoping it will hold my weight and lower myself slowly, turning my head a little so I can look down. I am only a few feet from the floor of the balcony, so I drop down trying to be as quiet as possible. Now what? The window seems to be locked so I will have to find another way in. I look down over the balcony at the pavement below. It's too far to drop down from here. I would probably break something if I tried it. I look to my left, nothing, no way down at all that way. I turn to my right and see a ledge below. If I step onto that I can get across to the roof of the porch that is the front entrance of the restaurant. I climb over the side of the balcony stretching my leg down and managing to put my right foot on the ledge which only comes out from the wall about three inches. There is also a ledge above me which I can just about reach if I stretch upwards. I hold on with my fingertips and slowly slide my toes along the lower ledge. I'm sweating and starting to panic as I shuffle across further. Just breathe I tell myself. I can do this, I'm almost there. A few more side steps take me right next to the porch roof. I step down onto the small flat roof and fall to my knees, breathing far too quickly. I wipe the sweat from my brow with the back of my hand and do my best to steady my breathing by closing my eyes and trying to clear my mind which should be virtually impossible right now but somehow, I manage it.

After a few minutes I am ready to move on. I lower myself down holding onto the edge of the porch and drop down to the ground. I look up. I can't quite believe I have just done that. I have actually got myself down from a rooftop! I feel like I could do anything right now, almost like I am invincible, like some kind of superhero or something. With my newfound confidence I walk around to the front door of the Chinese restaurant, open it and step inside.

"Come on in" I hear a familiar man's voice from over in the far corner of the restaurant. I make my way slowly over to the booth Tom and I always sit in when we eat here and see a man who I have seen many times before. He works here. He's the waiter who usually serves Tom and I, but he looks different from all the other times I have seen him. He is smartly dressed in what looks like traditional Chinese attire with a gold bird shape embroidered onto the material at the front instead of the usual white shirt and black trousers combo and has a serious look in his eyes but a smile on his face. "I have something for you" the waiter says and pushes a plate across the table towards me. On the plate is a single fortune cookie. I love these. Tom says the messages inside are a load of old rubbish and just superstition, but I actually think they mean something and can help a person in some way. "Take it" says the waiter. He stands, bows his head, looks up at me and then makes his way to the front door, opening it and closing it behind him. I run after him and open the door. He's gone, there's no sign of him outside. I don't know how he could have got away that quickly, he only left seconds ago. Why did he have to leave so soon anyway? I go back over to my favourite booth and pick up the fortune cookie. I have to know what it says inside, maybe there's a clue to what all this is about. I crack open the thin shell of the fortune cookie and take out a small rolled-up piece of paper. I put the shell of the cookie back down on the plate and unravel the small piece of paper and stare at the writing on it. I can't understand what it says. The writing is in a language that I don't recognise at all. I put the piece of paper in my pocket and leave the restaurant. It is getting late I presume, and I am so close to my old home that I think it is best that I stay there tonight. I can go back to the flat in the morning.

When I get to my mom's house I go around to the back and lift the large stone by the door to reveal the spare key. I unlock the back door and carefully open it trying to be as quiet as possible. I think everyone will be in bed even though I have no idea of the time, it just feels like the dead of night. Once inside I tiptoe towards the stairs and make my way up to my old bedroom. I close the door behind me and breathe a sigh of relief that no one has noticed I am here. I am too tired to try and explain myself tonight.

The sun is streaming through the gap in the curtains when I open my eyes from the deepest and most satisfying of sleeps. I feel like I have been asleep for hours and hours and am very well rested, probably because I'm back in my own bed, the bed which my body is so used to. How on earth am I going to explain to mom why I have woken up here instead of my new home? I open the bedroom door slightly and peer through the gap. I see mom and Beth. It looks like they are getting ready to go out. I'll just wait until they've gone to go downstairs then they'll never know I was here. I close the door and sit back down on my bed. I'm not sure I want to leave. I don't know if I'm ready for living with a man. Tom and I haven't been together for very long. Is it too soon and how well do we really know each other? I try to put those thoughts and questions out of my mind but being a terrible over thinker that is quite a feat.

I glance over to the dressing table mirror and see that the family photo is still stuck to it. How could I have missed that? I am sure I took the photo off the mirror and packed it away in the odds and ends box to take with me to the flat. It is not an odd or an end though as the photo is very precious to me. It depicts a time gone by when my dad was still alive and took us all on a lovely day out to a castle that I loved visiting. My dad was very interested in anything historical; castles, museums and even old book shops were right up his street. He used to say there was nothing like the feel of an antique whether it be a chair or a book if the object was aged it was interesting to him. I know what he meant, technology is great and everything but with old things you can almost feel the history, imagine who else has sat in that chair or turned the pages of that book years before you have. I pull the photo off the mirror and study it, looking at dad. I wish he was here right now so I could talk to him. We had great conversations, dad and I, about so many different things. I learned so much from that wonderful man, more than I have learned from anyone else.

I wipe a tear from my cheek and fold the photo over to put it in my pocket. On the back of the photo, the part that is now facing upwards there is what looks like a phone number scribbled in blue ink. I don't have my phone with me, it's at the flat and my mom doesn't have a landline. I must call this number. I feel like it's practically jumping off the back of the photo at me, willing me to dial the digits. I'm sure the number wasn't there before; I've never noticed it anyway and I am almost certain I put the photo in that last box that is now in the flat so I haven't got a clue how it could have got back here stuck to my mirror where it had been for years.

I need to get my phone, but I don't know how I am going to get back to the flat when I have no way of calling a taxi and haven't got any change for a bus. I run downstairs and open the front door thinking that I'll walk down to Mr Ramsbottom's shop and ask him to call a taxi for me but what I see outside surprises me, and I just stand there open mouthed. Tom's car is parked right outside the house. Tom opens the passenger side window and calls for me to get into the car. Ok, here we go. I guess I've got some explaining to do. I can't tell Tom the truth, he will think I am crazy but what can I say? "Missing home already, were you?" Tom asks as soon as I get into the car and close the door. "Um, yeah" I say nervously, "something like that." I look at Tom giving him a half smile to which he responds by rolling his eyes and saying nothing more about it which is so like him being a man of few words and a win-win for me being as I don't have to think of an excuse for not being at the flat.

I feel a bit of tension on the drive to the city but shrug it off as best I can and try not to over think the situation but of course failing miserably. I just need to get back and call that number on the back of the photo, I need to know who wrote it and why, at least this weird atmosphere between me and Tom isn't the only thing on my mind.

I grab my phone as soon as I get into the bedroom where I'd left it and try to unlock it. Oh no, it's dead, the battery's run out! I scrabble around in the drawer of the bedside table, but the charger isn't there. Tom's charger is different from mine so I can't use that. Where is mine? Hang on, I haven't charged my phone since I moved in here, so I have either left the charger at my mom's house or it's in the box I haven't unpacked yet, the odds and ends one. I reach up to the high shelf in the built-in wardrobe for the brown cardboard box and just about manage to inch it closer to the edge with my fingertips then it falls. Everything that was in the box goes everywhere then I see something sparkling on the thick cream carpet. It's the key pendant I had for my twenty- first birthday. I hadn't forgotten I had it, I just haven't dared wear it again after what did or possibly didn't really happen the last time I put the chain with the key attached to it around my neck.

I turn my attention back to finding my phone charger. There it is. It was in the box and is now on the floor by the bed. I grab the phone charger, plug it into the socket then the other end into my phone and wait. A few minutes should do it. Just enough charge to turn my phone on and make a quick call. I feel like this is the longest two minutes of my life as I sit on the floor next to my phone staring at it. "Everything ok?" Tom shouts from the living room, "I heard a bang." "I'm fine" I tell him, "I just dropped a box, nothing to worry about." I start putting things back in the box leaving the key until last. I pick it up and look at it. It really is quite beautiful, an almost black sapphire set into the bow of the silver key that seems to change colour as I hold it closer to the light. That should be long enough. I turn my phone on leaving it plugged in as it's probably only on a couple of percent battery and won't last long before it dies again if I take the charger out now. I pull the photo out of my pocket and call the phone number written on the back of it. It's ringing. My heart is pounding then someone answers. "The secret lies within the key." Whoever just said that hangs up. Is that it? What do they mean? I try calling the number again but this time there's just a recorded message saying that the number is unavailable. I sit on the floor propped up against the bed feeling stumped. I stare at the key as it lies daintily on the palm of my hand. What secret could the key hold? I can't think of anything that will even remotely help me work out what the voice on the other end of the phone meant so I wrap the fortune cookie paper around the key and the chain around the paper holding it in place then put it in my pocket.

Tom calls out to me saying he's been called into work as there's another emergency. There's a lot of that, Tom going out to save sick or hurt animals which I love about him, but I wonder if I am going to see much of him at all even though we are now living together. Just before he leaves Tom tells me that he has booked a table at a very expensive restaurant in town for tonight. "Ok great" I say then as Tom shuts the front door behind him, I wonder why we are going out tonight. Maybe he just wants to treat me to a special meal to make up for us not spending much time together lately.

I am alone. What to do now? I decide to go out and explore the city as I am on holiday from work at the moment to give me time to settle into my new surroundings, I should really make the most of it.

# CHAPTER 18

It's more pleasant than I imagined, walking down an inner-city road, all around me high-rise buildings. There's a different but still a kind of beauty in skyscrapers, high end shops that don't do price tags in the windows and boutique hotels. A few roads away from the flat I see a different sort of road across to my right. It looks like the side road is a cobble stone one like a lot of the roads back in the village. I can see pretty flowers in hanging baskets and painted shutters sticking out from windows. I must walk down that road, it looks far too interesting and quaint to ignore.

I cross over the busy main road and head straight for the cute cobble one opposite. Wow it's even prettier and more inviting up close. As soon as I step onto the cobbles, I feel good. A sense of warmth, happiness and comfort fills me inside and I strangely somehow feel like I have come home. I suppose it's because it reminds me so much of the village I grew up in, where my family still lives and of my dad who loved little olde-worlde places like this. We visited many small villages and market towns over the years as a family, all of us together. It's not really been the same since dad died. I wish he was here to see this; he would have felt the same way I do about it; I know he would have.

There's a florist with an abundance of gorgeously coloured blooms outside and inside the shop. The lady inside elaborately arranging flowers smiles at me as I walk past, and I smile back. Opposite there's a tiny old fashioned looking pub called The Journey Inn. I could do with a drink, so I cross the street looking both ways to check for traffic. That's strange, there's a wall where the street starts, where it connects to the main road. I walk back down the street towards the wall and touch it. Sure enough, it is made of solid brick. How did I get through the wall to stand on this street? This wall was not there before. For some reason I don't feel like panicking about it and just accept it and shrug it off, I don't really know why. I walk back towards the pub and make my way inside.

There are a few people sat at small wooden tables sipping curious looking drinks, red and green liquids filling elaborate looking glass goblets. They each turn to look at who has entered the pub then look back down as soon as they see me. A friendly looking man says "hello" from behind the bar. "What can I get you?" He asks me. I walk across to the bar wondering about the mysterious looking drinks other people seem to be enjoying. "What are they drinking?" I ask glancing across at some of the people sitting down at tables. "The drinks look different here huh?" The barman questions me smiling again. "Yes, they do but do you mind if I ask, where exactly is 'here'?" I say, puzzled. "Welcome to Forever" he answers. Now I am even more confused. "What is 'Forever'?" I ask. "We are paused here, suspended between the seconds in time" the barman says. "What do you mean?" I ask, intrigued. "We are not in the present, the past or the future. This is another time, one where you can stay infinitely if you choose to" he explains. "I can't stay" I say. "As lovely as it is here, I don't want to be just stuck in between moments in time forever, I can't." The barman looks at me, shakes his head and sighs, "ok then, you'll need to see the professor. He'll be in the bookshop where he always is." "Ok thanks" I say then make my way back outside.

Now I need to find the bookshop. I turn right and walk up the street away from the wall which I unwittingly walked right through. I pass small houses with brightly coloured doors and matching wooden shutters on windows. Everything is so perfect here. It would be easy to stay. It feels nice being here in this place in between times. Maybe being stuck is the answer.

Maybe I should just stop. I could be this age forever and never get old or ill. It is a tempting thought, but I know that I can't settle here, it wouldn't be right somehow. I continue past house after house, each one looking like as the last apart from different coloured doors and shutters. Finally, I see it. The sign above the shop says 'Ye Olde Book Shop'. I cross the cobbles and stand outside the very small, quaint looking bookshop and peek through the window. It's quite dark inside so I can't see much then a face appears at the window and makes me jump! "Come in" I hear a man's low and slightly shaky voice say. I catch my breath and step inside the shop. "Are you the professor?" I ask when I see a little old man with wild curly grey hair and a long pointy beard clutching a well-worn walking stick. "That is what they call me" says the professor. I clear my throat and tell him that the barman sent me. "I see. So, you'll want to be getting back then" the professor says looking over his thinly framed spectacles directly at me. "Yes" I say, "can you tell me how to do that?" The professor replies "you already have the answer." I have absolutely no idea what he means by that but just watch him as he hobbles over slowly to a ladder that has been propped up against a huge bookcase. "You'll have to go up" the professor says looking up the ladder. For some reason I don't feel the need to question him, I feel like this old man is trustworthy enough, so I walk across to the ladder and start climbing.

I look up. I can't see an end to the ladder now that I am climbing up it as if it is infinite. I look at the books to the left, right, above and below me. There must be hundreds of them, possibly thousands as the bookshelf appears to grow and get bigger and bigger. I see a book that stands out amongst the rest. The book is very thick and looks as if it is made from solid silver. I reach to pull it out from between two less interesting looking brown books. The silver book is lighter than I had expected it to be, I can hold it easily in one hand as I hold onto the ladder with the other. Feeling that perhaps I have found what I went up the ladder for I start to climb back down only to find that within seconds I am stepping back onto the floor. How can I be back down on solid ground already? I was up so high only a moment ago. I suppose anything is possible in this place.

There's a small mahogany table with a stool next to it in front of me so I set the book down on the table and sit, pulling the stool in closer underneath me. The silver book is so shiny, it looks as if it has just been made, never touched by another human hand and now I have the honour of opening the cover to reveal the secrets that are held inside. I open the book and scan the first page. There's a diagram on it of a key and all the different parts are labelled. I study the picture of the key and then it occurs to me, this bears more than just a passing resemblance to the key in my pocket, my key pendant. Underneath is a small paragraph which reads:

One key can unlock many doors.          One key can unlock the past and the future.    One key holds a mystery which only one can solve.

I pull the key out of my pocket, still wrapped with the fortune cookie paper and lie the paper down on the table, flattening it as best I can. I place the key above the diagram on the first page of the silver book. I glance at my key then the illustration and back again. I look at the end of the pin on my silver key and notice it looks like a tiny carriage bolt. I pick the key up and see if the end will unscrew. The bolt is quite tight, but I persevere with trying to unscrew it until eventually it loosens slightly, and I can indeed unscrew the tiny silver bolt. I take the smooth headed carriage bolt out of the pin of the key and place it down on the table. It looks like there is something inside the key. I need something to get whatever it is out. Tweezers would be useful right now. I get up and look all around me. Where has the professor gone? He was here before I climbed up the ladder. I must have been so enamoured with the silver book, wondering what was written inside that I didn't give the old man a second thought. I guess I am on my own in the bookshop now.

I start looking around for something to retrieve whatever is inside the key. There's a desk across the other side of the room that might have something useful on it, so I walk over to it to look. On closer inspection there are only books, pens and a small lamp with a pull cord attached underneath the shade. I pull the cord and turn on the lamp which in doing so reveals an arrow that's glowing and pointing towards the back of the shop. I grab the book, putting the small piece of paper inside, screw the bolt back into the end of the key and put it in my pocket then head in the direction the glowing arrow is pointing.

There's a door at the back of the room and nothing else. I turn around expecting to see the bookshelves, the table, the desk and the shop window but all I see is an empty room which looks very different now everything is gone. There's no handle or doorknob but there is a keyhole in what appears to now be the only way out of this room. I pull the key out of my pocket and try it in the lock. It fits. I turn the key and the door opens. I take the key back out of the hole and put it safely back into my pocket. I push the door open and step out onto a pavement. I close the door behind me and look around. I am astonished to find that I am back in the city, exactly where I was when I first spotted the cobble street except the street is gone, vanished it seems and nothing but another office building stands where Forever was. I wonder if it moves. Maybe you can only pass through to it in the place that it is in at that moment in time once then another time you must go somewhere else to find it. Maybe it finds you. I've got a feeling I will never see that particular street again and I feel quite sad at the thought. I miss being there already. At least now I am back in the city I can go back to the flat and find something to get whatever is inside the key out of it.

I look down quite a bit out of habit when I am walking along. Sometimes that means I bump into people or maybe the odd lamppost, but I am fascinated with the thought of what I might find on the ground. There's usually the odd coin, maybe a pretty leaf in the autumn and there is always litter which I pick up and put in the nearest bin as I can't stand the pavements or anywhere for that matter being littered. I walk along looking ahead for now then to my left into shop windows with their expensive looking clothes, electronics and jewellery. I then look down at the pavement to see what treasures I might discover and spot a pretty hair grip. I can't resist picking it up but then feel bad for whoever lost such a beautiful piece of what can only be described I think as hair jewellery. The grip is long and silver with multi coloured stones on the end you would see when positioned correctly on a person's crowning glory. I put the grip ever so slightly guiltily into my hair and continue walking on down the city street.

There's what looks like could be a park up ahead which I decide to make my way towards. It's nice that there can still be a haven of greenery in the middle of a big city I think to myself as I am walking. I am excited to see grass, trees and possibly even a pond, fingers crossed. The black cast iron gates are open, so I pass through them, entering the park. I start walking along a small winding path that looks like it goes all the way through this green oasis. To me it is almost like I have been traipsing through a desert desperate for a drink and now I have found water. I know that probably sounds dramatic, but I can't help it. I am just so in love with the countryside that I am not at all sure I can live without it.

As I get further into the park, I spot a bench. There's a golden plaque on the back rest of the elegant black metal bench which reads 'sit and ponder'. "I will do, thank you very much" I say out loud and take a seat. I lay the silver book on my lap and open the front cover. I take the fortune cookie paper out of the book and hold it tightly so it doesn't blow away in the breeze. I turn over the first page to see what else is either written or drawn in this unusual looking book. The second page is just plain paper, there's nothing on it. I turn the next page then the next and start flicking through the whole of the book. There is nothing else on any of the other pages, just the diagram of the key and the three lines of writing. I don't understand this. Why would anyone write or draw on only one page of a book and then leave the rest empty? It seems a shame, a waste of a beautifully bound and covered book. I go back to the first page and read the paragraph again.

One key can unlock many doors.
One key can unlock the past and the future.
One key holds a mystery which only one can solve.

The more I read it the more I feel like those three lines have been written for me. I can't really explain it, but it seems to mean something to me especially as my key is exactly the same as the one illustrated in this book. I turn my attention to the key and remember that I found something inside it earlier. Of course, that's it, the grip! I slide the bejewelled grip that I found on the pavement back in the city out of my hair. I unscrew the bolt out of the end of the key and place it down on the book. I open the grip and try gently to push it into the pin of the key. It fits inside so I wiggle it around as best I can and slowly pull out a small piece of paper. It's the same size and shape as the other one I have, the one that came out of the fortune cookie. The paper I have just fished out of the key also has the same style of writing on it as the fortune cookie one. I don't understand what either inscription says. It's a foreign language or maybe some sort of symbolism that I have no idea how to read. I put the paper from the key on top of the other one to roll them back up together then notice something. The words start to make sense. With one piece of paper on top of the other I can read what has been written.

The answers are in the past and in the future.
Use the key.

The past and the future, how can the answers be in both and the answers to what anyway? I'm not sure where to use the key but I have a feeling I will be finding out soon. I guess I should be heading back now. It has been quite an interesting, not to mention exciting and exhausting day and I need to go back to the flat, have a long hot relaxing bath then get ready for my date with Tom tonight.

# CHAPTER 19

This is the fanciest restaurant I've ever seen let alone eaten in. The ceiling is extremely high and the crystals in the chandeliers catch the light as they dangle down suspended by extremely thin threads that are hardly visible to the naked eye. This place reminds me of somewhere somehow. I think I dreamt of being somewhere like this a long time ago but as with many of my dreams it feels more like a vague memory. A very smartly dressed waiter greets Tom and I and asks us to follow him over to our table.

The chairs are covered in luxurious deep purple velvet and as I sit down, I sink into mine, it's so comfortable. The table has a glass top and intricately carved, highly polished wooden legs. I feel quite overwhelmed sitting here if I'm honest. It's not really me all this finesse and refinement. I feel a bit out of place, but I know that Tom has always been used to this kind of luxury, he did grow up in a castle after all. "Wow Tom, this place is amazing" I say looking all around and taking in the beauty and atmosphere of the restaurant. "This place once belonged to a count or a duke, something like that" Tom tells me. "It was a long time ago, I'm not sure when but apparently the royal owner threw parties regularly to try and find his true love." Tom scoffs "well that's what I heard anyway. Pretty sad really that he never found her." "That is sad" I say, the dream coming back to me, hitting a nerve somewhere deep inside. My emotions stir and I feel hurt without having the slightest clue as to why. "Anyway" Tom carries on, "we're not here to talk about some bloke from years ago that probably didn't even exist, we're here to talk about us Alex." Just then the waiter comes over with what looks like a bottle of very expensive champagne and pours a little in both mine and Tom's glass flutes while classical music plays in the background. Tom picks up his glass and says, "to us." I pick my glass up and chink it against Tom's, "to us" I say back, smiling at him. Tom smiles back at me with a slight glint in his eyes then gets up and puts his hand in his pocket. He pulls out a small black box and gets down on one knee. Tom opens the box and says "Alexandra Rose Heeton, will you marry me?" There inside the box surrounded by white satin sits a gold ring set with a huge sapphire. The ring is stunning, I love it! Caught up in the moment I say, "yes Tom, I will marry you." Tom takes the ring out of the box and places it on my finger. It fits perfectly and looks so pretty, the precious stone a glorious deep blue. I stare at the sapphire and start to daydream, sort of getting lost and feeling like I'm falling into something. "Alex, are you ok?" I snap out of my trance like state to see Tom with a concerned look on his face. "I'm fine, I was just daydreaming. This ring is so perfect" I reply, telling Tom only half the truth.

The rest of the evening is nice. For starter we have a very fragrant clear soup that is served in small fine bone china bowls then for the fish course a lovely lobster dish. Main course is rib of beef with a red wine jus and for pudding (which is the best bit) a trio of mini desserts, chocolate pot, mixed berry mousse and my favourite lemon drizzle cake. The champagne has been flowing. I feel tipsy and lightheaded but happy too. I am engaged! I am actually going to get married and the man I am marrying couldn't be more perfect really. Life is good but I still can't rest until I find out what the key and fortune cookie message means.

I lie in bed after getting back from our eventful evening out thinking about my life now. I don't think it will be a very long engagement as Tom likes to get things done and dusted, no messing about. He is extremely organised and likes to know exactly what he is doing and what he's got planned. I'm surprised he copes with going out on so many emergencies to help sick animals with the way he is. I guess he just puts the animals first. I smile thinking about how selfless Tom can be.

The next morning, I wake up alone. Tom has already gone to work. There's a note on the bedside table. I reach across and pick it up then read what has been written on the note and smile. The note simply says, 'love you'. I lift my left hand up and gaze at my beautiful engagement ring. I need to organise a party then there's wedding dress shopping, deciding on a venue for the ceremony and the reception not to mention who to invite. I have so much to think about that I almost forget about the key. It's at the back of my mind though, firmly fixed there and I think that I need to find out what it all means before I can fully concentrate on wedding planning. I guess Tom will play a big part in the organising of everything anyway as that is what he is good at, and he knows planning anything is not one of my strengths. I have decided one thing though that I will not be backing down on no matter how much Tom may try and change my mind, the place we are going to get married in, the church in my old village. It's perfect. It's where my mom and dad got married and my grandma and granddad before them. Yes, it must be there. Tom can pick the venue for the reception.

What to do today then, I wonder as I get out of bed stretching and yawning then realise my head hurts from too much fizz last night. I make my way downstairs to the kitchen and find some painkillers in a small box in one of the cupboards, a kind of first aid kit for situations such as my hangover. I fill a glass with water and take two tablets hoping they will be enough to do the trick and get rid of the thumping in my head. I drink the rest of the water, knowing that will also help to make me feel better and open the fridge suddenly feeling very hungry despite eating a four-course meal last night. Hmm I really need to do a food shop. There isn't much in this massive American style fridge that I bet cost a fortune. I suppose I may as well go out for breakfast then.

I get dressed into my usual comfortable attire of t-shirt and jeans and head out after grabbing my small brown worn leather bag that I had already put the papers and key safely inside along with my phone, purse and keys to the flat. I don't know where the silver book is. I am sure I put it away in my odds and ends box in the wardrobe, but I looked for it when I got back last night, and it wasn't there. I'm starting to think that I never really put it in there and that I had imagined it. If I had imagined it though, how would I know about the key? I couldn't have just worked out how to open it to discover the note inside could I? What about the pretty road with the cobbles, the place called Forever, was that real? I'm not sure what is or isn't real after yesterday then I glance at my engagement ring and think of Tom and getting married, that's real, that is my reality.

I shut the door to the flat behind me and walk across the corridor to the lift. I press the gold button next to the lift to call it and wait. The lift makes a funny creaking sound as it comes up to the top floor which is strange as I'm sure it didn't make a sound like that before. The lift doors open so I step inside and press the button with a G on it. The lift jerks as if it's stuck and trying to move at first then it starts to get going but after a few seconds is speeding up way too much. It's going too fast. "Stop, stop!" I shout and with that the lift jerks this time to a stop and the doors fly open.

I am certainly not where I should be right now. I should be on the ground floor of the apartment building looking directly at Pete the security man but instead, well I don't know. I'm not sure where I am. I step out of the lift into a corridor. It's not an ultra-modern high gloss one like the ones in the apartment building but a more traditional looking one, maybe Victorian in style. In front of me are two doors. Both doors look the same; very old wooden front doors painted red. I walk towards the door on the left. There is a plaque on it which says 'past'. I look at the door on the right. The plaque on that one says 'future'. Do I need to choose which door to open? Where do I want to go? Maybe I won't choose either. I think I'll explore this corridor and see if there is another way. I turn around to where the lift should be, but it's gone now and there's just another plain wall in place of the lift which looks like it could do with a lick of paint. "Ok right" I say out loud, turn to my right and start walking. There are lit candles in holders attached to the walls every now and then lighting my way but nothing else. There is no sound, no sign of life apart from my footsteps on the ground and my heart beating faster and faster the further I get along this dimly lit and seemingly never-ending corridor of curiosity. It goes on and on and I wonder if it will ever change or end, this corridor of walls and candles, then it does. Without warning suddenly, I am falling, down, down then I land with a thud. I open my eyes having had them squeezed tightly shut on the journey to wherever I am now and look around. I am in the lift again. The doors open and I'm back facing the two red doors. I step out of the lift and look to my right. There's another corridor which looks the same as the one I have already been down. Worth a try I guess I think as I start walking. I'm not sure why I feel determined not to try one of the doors. Maybe I don't want to be made to choose. Maybe I want to be free to make my own decision and maybe I choose neither door.

This corridor is different from the last one. Gone are the candles now although I'm sure they were there when I was standing outside the lift. In place of candles there are tiny spotlights dotted around which reminds me of stars in a clear night sky. The walls are shiny and white. I can almost see my reflection in them as I continue to walk down this brightly lit corridor. What if I get to the end and the same thing happens as before? I turn around and start walking back thinking that maybe it isn't worth feeling that thud again. Surely, I should see the red doors again soon and the other corridor, but I don't. There is nothing but white gloss walls and spotlights now. I turn back and it's the same. It's all the same in here. I start to panic. How do I get out of here? I shout "help!" hoping someone somewhere will hear me. I close my eyes and scream. Then I hear a voice. It's faint but I can make out that whoever the voice belongs to is calling my name.

"Alex. Alex." I open my eyes to see Beth staring down at me. I sit up. How am I on the floor? "Are you ok?" Beth asks me. "I'm not sure" I reply honestly. "Where am I?" I ask my sister. "You're in the park Alex. I found you lying on the path." I start sobbing uncontrollably feeling as if I am losing my mind and my grip on reality. Beth throws her arms around me and holds me tightly telling me that everything is going to be ok. When I start to calm down, I begin to explain to Beth about what's been going on with everything. The reoccurring dreams that feel more like memories, the key I had for my twenty first birthday, the place called Forever, the corridor and even that Henry the cat's real name is Exodus, and he is also a bird who grows and carries me to different places. It all sounds crazy saying it out loud, but I feel relieved talking to someone about my strange experiences at last. "Ok" Beth says calmly. "Show me the key and the message." I pull the key and the papers out of my pocket and pass them to my sister. She looks at the key and passes it back to me then unravels the papers. "Believe in yourself for only you can do it. You will find a way, be strong" Beth seems to read while looking at the small thin notes. "That's not what it says" I say feeling perplexed. Beth hands the papers back to me. I put one on top of the other and hold them up so my concerned looking younger sister can see them. "Alex" Beth says looking right into my eyes like she's searching for something. She's getting worried now, I can tell.

"They say what I just read out to you." I look at the notes again and read out what I see. "The answers are in the past and the future. Use the key." "But Alex, that's not what is written on those pieces of paper, and you don't even need to put them together like you did, you can just read what is written on each one" Beth says now looking more worried than ever. Am I going crazy? I must be because I don't see what she sees. I start crying again, feeling that I am spiralling into blackness. This is what it must feel like to lose your mind and I don't know what to do about it. "Come on, let's get you to the house" Beth says in a soft, gentle, comforting tone whilst helping me to my feet.

Beth and I get back to mom's house and I head up to my old room for a rest. I lie down on my comfy old bed and close my eyes which are swollen and sore from all the tears I have cried. I need to rest them and try to get some sleep. I am just about drifting off to the land of dreams when I hear a meow. I open my puffy, sticky eyes to see Henry lying on the pillow right next to me. "Oh Henry what am I going to do? Beth doesn't believe me, she thinks I'm going crazy I am sure, and I can't risk telling anyone else about what's been happening, they'll probably have me sectioned. Am I crazy? Have I gone mad?" Henry just looks at me with his beautifully odd eyes. Maybe that's just it, perhaps I have gone mad. I am talking to a cat after all, asking him questions as if he were a person and might have the answers. I'll make an appointment with the doctor and tell him that I think I might be mentally ill and need help.

I hear voices downstairs, people talking in serious tones, but I can't quite make out what they are saying. I get up off the bed, stepping onto my old bedroom floor with bare feet and, feeling a chill pass through me like someone has walked over my grave, I tentatively make my way downstairs. Mom, Beth and Tom are sitting down in the living room busily talking but fall silent as soon as they notice me. "Alex" Tom starts, "we all think it would be a good idea to get you some help." Mom continues, "Tom has booked you in for a few weeks at a private unit. It sounds very nice, and you'll be well looked after, I am sure." "What do you mean a unit?" I ask my mom, feeling confused. "You have been saying some really strange stuff Alex and when I found you in such a state, I didn't know what to do so I called Tom then mom came back and we all discussed what to do" says Beth, a tear welling in her eye as she looks at me and holds my hand. I feel angry that they all decided to talk about me behind my back. I know I sound like a crazy person but I'm not a hundred percent sure I really am mad and anyway, if I was insane surely, I wouldn't be questioning in my own head whether I was or wasn't, I would just be.

Henry slinks into the living room and sits down loyally at my feet. "Henry, tell them that I am not crazy. Change into Exodus and tell them, please" I say desperately. I do sound like a crazy person now. I know I do. Everyone just stands staring at me. Henry has a blank expression on his fluffy face, and I wonder what is real anymore. Maybe Henry is in fact just a cat and perhaps I should go to this unit place and try to reclaim my sanity. "Come on Alex, it won't be for long. I'm sure you'll be back to normal in no time. You're probably just stressed. Moving away from home must be difficult for you and then there's a wedding to plan. It hasn't helped losing your job either I guess" Tom says in a caring way. As I walk out of the house with my family, I wonder what Tom meant by losing my job. I'm on holiday from work, that's all. I get into Tom's car and soon realise that mom and Beth aren't coming with us, they just stand at the garden gate watching me leave.

After about an hour's drive that has felt much longer because Tom and I haven't spoken a word to each other on the journey, we pull up at a very modern looking, almost futuristic square building. "We're here" Tom says then gets out of the car, walks around quickly to the passenger side and opens the door for me. I step out of the car and study the exterior of what is going to be home for the next few weeks. I'm scared. I feel tears welling in my eyes just about to spill out and over my flushed cheeks. I swallow hard trying to push my emotions down and not show my fiancé how upset I am about all this. He might think I am more mentally ill than he clearly already does. Tom takes hold of my arm gently and leads me towards the front door of the unit.

# CHAPTER 20

As soon as I step inside, I smell disinfectant. It's quite overpowering and I almost gag. My sense of smell seems heightened as are my emotions now. I don't want to be here, but I don't think I have much choice in the matter with Tom obviously determined to get me the help that he thinks I need and seeming to know that this is the place that is going to sort my head out. I guess I'm just going to have to suck it up and grin and bear it here for the next two weeks.

Everywhere is white as I look around the unit, bright glossy white and I have a strong sense of déjà vu right now. I have been here before; I swear I have but I just don't when or how I could have been. A middle-aged lady with short curly auburn coloured hair greets us with a friendly (if a little over friendly) smile and introduces herself as nurse Wren. I don't think I have ever heard a name like that, it's very unusual. Tom says a quick goodbye and kisses me on the head like you might do a child as you usher them off through the school gates, and I am left with a feeling of being patronised and abandoned all in one. He could have at least said a proper fair well to me. After all, Tom won't see me for a few weeks. Maybe he doesn't want to prolong the agony of having to walk away and leave me here when he knows he will go back home to an empty flat. I bet he's worried, he must be, and he is only doing this because he cares about me, and he doesn't want me to completely lose my mind. He's trying to fix me. Do I even need fixing though? I'm not sure if I do or I don't.

The extremely jolly nurse Wren leads me down a long shiny corridor to my room. It's very white and shiny and spotless as it is everywhere inside this place. I notice something strange about my room as I look around. There are no joins, no breaks in the decor, no tiles, nothing like that. It's like the room is one continuous glossy square but slightly oval shape with smooth edges. It doesn't change or finish anywhere apart from when the perfectly smooth surface that the walls and ceiling in one is meets the opening I walked through to get into this odd little bubble of a bedroom. The door has a seal around it. The oval shape that is the door fits tightly into the oval opening and there is no handle on the inside. Great, I'm trapped. I feel my heart beating faster, the blood pumping through my veins with more haste as panic starts to rise. A knock at the door brings my focus back and seems to snap me out of my imminent hyperventilation. I take a deep breath, clear my throat and say "come in." The door opens and a smartly dressed man with silvery thinning hair, black heavy framed glasses and a short pointy beard steps into to my bubble room. "Hello Alexandra. My name is Doctor Blunt. I will be looking after you while you are here at the unit" the man says quietly but in a controlled and confident manner. "Hi doctor" I say nervously. "Why isn't there a handle on the inside of the door?" I ask the petite but somewhat intimidating man suspiciously. Doctor Blunt smiles and scoffs a little, "it's very easy to get lost when you are not used to where you are." I don't buy that for one minute. I'm not stupid, he's hiding something, and I have already decided that I don't trust this so-called doctor one bit. I'll play along like a good little patient for now until I find out what is really going on here. "Ok, I just wondered" I say with a small smile which is all I can manage. "I really need to go to the toilet, which way is it?" I ask Doctor Blunt. "Nurse Wren will escort you there Alexandra and when you come back, we will have more of a chat" the creepy doctor says then steps back out of my bubble room and calls the nurse.

Nurse Wren holds my arm as we walk down the white corridor. I don't know why she feels the need to do that, I'm not about to run off and try to escape although to be quite honest the thought had crossed my mind more than once already, this place is giving me the almighty creeps. "Two minutes" nurse Wren says when we get to the ladies' toilet. I am shocked that I have a time limit but say nothing not wanting to question the rules and arouse suspicion that I don't think this place is quite right and head towards a cubicle. I don't even really need to go to the toilet, I just wanted to get away from that weird little doctor and have a further look around. It all looks the same. This room is basically the same as my bedroom except there are toilet cubicles and wash basins instead of a bed and a small table. I sit on the toilet with my head in my hands wondering how I am going to get through the next few weeks inside this uncomfortably quiet and controlled unit. I don't even want to be here one more minute. Surely, they can't hold me against my will unless I have been sectioned. I can't see how that could have happened so quickly and without seeing my GP. I don't know what time it is as I'm not wearing a watch, and Tom kept my phone as he said mobiles are banned here. This is all too weird. Nothing about my situation here feels right. I know I'm not crazy and that there is a place, a wonderful place that may as well be a million miles away from here called Forever and right now, I wish I had chosen to stay there.

"Time's up" I hear nurse Wren call out to me. "Ok, just washing my hands" I lie. I exit the toilet and smile as sweetly as I can while secretly trying to hatch a plan of escape, the cogs in my mind connecting and turning, different thoughts crossing over each other, trying to connect, hoping that an idea will come and that no one puts a spanner in the works and the machine that is the thought process in my brain breaks down.

At teatime I am led by the same overly cheerful nurse as usual to a small canteen with five white tables in it, two white chairs at each. All the chairs are taken already by patients apart from one near the window which must have been left for me. I walk across to the small round table by the window gaining a few passing glances along the way and sit down on the empty chair opposite my new dining partner, a young slim woman with long white-blonde hair. The woman doesn't look up at me and instead just stares at the table with her head down. "Hi" I say trying to sound friendly and upbeat. The depressed looking woman doesn't look up or answer me. "My name is Alex, what's yours?" I ask in the hope that my date for this lunch time will indeed be capable of some form of conversation and will not continue to leave me hanging. A man glances across at me from the next table then looks over to where nurse Wren is standing as if to check she has not noticed him speaking to another patient before looking back my way. "She can't answer you, she's mute" he tells me in a very hushed tone which makes it difficult to understand but I get there by mostly lip reading. "Ok thanks" I say to the man opposite after a quick check to make sure nurse Wren is busy with another patient and not eyeballing us. The kind looking old man smiles and looks back down at his table. As I look around the canteen, I realise that everyone is looking down at their tables and not talking. That is strange, I wonder why. A tall woman with a severe bobbed hair cut dressed head to toe in black shiny clothes that I guess is some sort of uniform walks over to my table and says that I should look down too. I look down even though I don't want to which make my blood boil inside my veins, but I know I need to keep playing the game, just for now anyway.

I see a young man wearing a white uniform like nurse Wren's coming into the canteen carrying a tray of cups as I look up slightly hoping no one will notice then quickly look back down fully again as the man makes his way over to my table. Two cups are placed down on the table in front of me. One cup is filled halfway with what looks like plain water and the other has two tablets in it. "Take these" the man says. "What are they?" I ask. "Your food and your medication" my sort of waiter I suppose says looking slightly puzzled, as if I should have already known what they were. Ok a tablet instead of proper food, that really isn't normal. "I'd like to speak to my doctor please" I say to the man, "Doctor Blunt." The man puts two more cups down on the table and walks away holding his tray with yet more cups of water and drugs on out in front of him to continue to distribute to the other lab rats in here. I can't do this, I need answers. I stand up and say loudly "Doctor Blunt, I want to speak to Doctor Blunt!" Two burly men suddenly run in and grab my arms. I scream and kick out "let me go, let me go" I shout repeatedly until I feel a prick on the left side of my neck, and everything goes black.

I wake up and look around. I can hardly move but at least I am conscious now. I am in my bubble room lying flat on my back on a very uncomfortable single bed and there's a funny taste in my mouth along with an unusual yet somewhat familiar scent filling the atmosphere in here. It's not exactly an unpleasant taste or smell, just a bit strange, it's almost sweet and not like anything I've ever tasted or inhaled before. I manage to sit up, gaining a little bit of strength back then moments later wishing I had stayed lying down as my head hurts and now the room is spinning. It must be the aftereffects of whatever the hell those men injected me with. How dare they do that to me! I feel totally violated to be honest. They could have done anything to me when I was out cold and I wouldn't have a clue about it, I was utterly defenceless. I am going to be putting a in a formal complaint about the way I have been treated when I get out of this hellhole, which, I might add, cannot come soon enough. Ok, I must be clever here. I really need to play along with them now, no more outbursts from me and back to being the good little patient once again. Maybe I can win their trust back like that and then find a way out of here.

The door to my room opens and in steps the doctor with his

patronising smile and his silly little pointy beard. I almost let out a snigger, he is so funny looking really, now I think about it, but I manage to just about stop myself, I have to let him think that I respect him. I clear my throat, smile a sweetly as I can and say, "Hello doctor, I'm feeling much better now." Doctor Blunt scoffs a little, looks down then straight at me "that's good, I am glad that what we had to give you helped, you were hysterical. You had to be calmed down." I smile again, feeling like an alter ego is about to take over my body at any moment and rip the silly little man's head off. "I understand why you had to do what you did now, I've had time to think and calm down" I lie. "You are all just doing your best for me, and I really appreciate your efforts to make me well again. "That's very good news Alexandra. I'm glad to hear we are on the same page" Doctor Blunt says and touches my shoulder which sends a horrible shiver down my spine and freaks me out, but I keep the fake smile plastered across my face, I need to wait this out. I take my night-time tablet as I'm supposed to and fall asleep quickly after lights out.

The next morning, I wash, get dressed into my simple hospital outfit consisting of plain grey trousers and an equally dreary shapeless grey tunic top then press the button by the door which basically means I am asking to be let out of my room. Nurse Wren opens the thin oval door and escorts me down the white corridor to the canteen where breakfast is being served. I have no idea what time it is, but it must be quite early as I look out of the window and see that the sun is still quite low in the sky and it's not broad daylight yet. I ask Nurse Wren for the time, but she says it's the unit's policy that patients don't know the exact time of day during their stay here.

Breakfast turns out to be just as interesting as tea was last night. On the menu are two tablets again, one white, one pink. I don't know which tablet is meant to be the food and which is the medication, but I don't suppose it matters as I'm going to have to take both of them. After around ten minutes I'd say, everyone is taken out of the canteen, one by one presumably back to their rooms and that's it for the next few hours. No chatting, no reading or watching TV. There's nothing at all to do here. I just sit in my room with only my thoughts for company. It's not like I can even go back to sleep for a bit because the lights are on and don't get turned off until night-time. This is depressing. I thought this place was meant to make a person better mentally, but I feel as if I could go out of my mind with boredom and lack of social interaction. I stare at the wall thinking, hoping, desperately trying to put a plan of action together to escape from this mostly mundane and occasionally abusive cult like place. I try and try, not coming up with anything, like my mind is a blank page in a book and that the author has writers block, or their pen has run out of ink. Maybe whatever that medication is has affected my thinking.

The next few days are the same as the previous ones. Everyone does the same thing. It's like we are all robots and not allowed to think outside the box and question anything. I thought there would be some form of therapy, but I haven't had a counselling session yet. I wish I had my key. I'm not sure why but for some reason I think it might help me. My key is in a locker by the reception desk. Everything that I came in with is in that locker and I can't get access to any of it. I sit on the floor propped up against the bed and start to cry. I am upset, hurt and afraid then something builds in me, and my emotions change to anger and outrage. How could they do this to me? There's nothing wrong with me. I know I am not crazy, and I know that everywhere I have been and everything I have experienced was real. The dreams I've always had weren't only dreams but are memories, I know that now too. I think about the key. I picture it being in my hand. I feel my emotions building and building, swirling around throughout my body and mind like a tornado is forming then I pass out.

When I come to, I feel terrible. My head hurts and I feel like I've just done ten rounds with a professional boxer and lost badly. I feel something in my hand. I'm holding something. It can't be, it just can't, can it? I open my tightly clasped hand slowly and gasp in sheer amazement as I see the only thing that is worth anything at all to me right now, my beautiful silver key! Even though I feel bruised and sore I pull myself up and sit on the edge of the metal framed single bed. I stare down at my key. I can't believe I've got it in my hand. It was in the locker. I imagined I had it and now I have. I laugh out loud, I can't help it, I am so happy right now, so excited. If I can do this, then what else can I do? I must need to unlock something, something that will surely help me get out of here. I hear the door opening and close my hand. These people cannot see the key. I need to keep it hidden. I lie down on the bed just before Doctor Blunt enters the room. "Good news Alexandra" says my funny little captor, "as you have done so well so far you will be allowed to spend some time in the courtyard after dinner." I didn't even know there was a courtyard here, but this is something to look forward to. It might be my chance to escape.

I am really surprised when I step into the courtyard. It's quite beautiful with flowers all around the edge, benches to sit on and a fountain in the middle. I sit next to a woman who looks like she's in her thirties maybe and say "hi." She just looks at me briefly, smiles then looks back toward the fountain, seeming to be in some sort of trance. "How long have you been here?" I ask the woman. "Too long" she says without blinking or taking her eyes off the fountain. She suddenly starts rambling in some sort of gibberish, just staring straight ahead then stops suddenly and grabs my arm firmly. The woman looks deeply into my eyes and says, "the past will lead you to the future." "What? What do you mean?" I ask, trying to prize her hand from my arm as she is clutching me now so tightly that it is starting to hurt. She lets go, places her hands on her lap, smiles at me and says, "beautiful here, isn't it?" I'm not sure what just happened but it can't be a coincidence. It can't be just some crazy woman spouting rubbish, what she said must be a message.

I need to find a way back to the past. How far back will I go though? I don't really care as long as it's more than four days and being in this place hasn't happened yet. I see something out of the corner of my eye as I am looking at the fountain with only my wild thoughts for company. I turn my head to my right slightly and notice something moving in the flower bed. I get up off the white plastic bench to take a closer look at what could be making the plants rustle like that, glancing back to make sure I haven't been seen by any of the nurses. The coast looks clear so I step closer to investigate what could be causing the movement of the brightly coloured flowers. I hear more rustling and I'm sure I hear purring. There must be a cat that lives here, presumably as a mouser. I wonder if the cat is friendly and will let me stroke it, I think to myself as I part the flowers gently. "Henry?" I can't believe it, it's my cat. Henry is here! He must have changed into Exodus and flown here then changed back into a cat to not arouse any suspicion. Henry looks at me, meows then walks away from me. I follow him instantly and find myself crawling through blooms of purple, pink, blue and yellow. The perfume from all the different flowers is amazing as I carry on following Henry, right on his tail, I don't want to lose him. This must be a very deep border of flowers as I seem to have been crawling on my hands and knees on the soil for at least five minutes now and Henry still isn't slowing down. Finally, I see an end to the foliage ahead but as I crawl out the other side of the border, I realise I am not outside the unit anymore.

There is a button on a plain brick wall in front of me. I press it and hear something moving. It sounds like a lift going up or down, I can't tell which. Doors appear out of nowhere right in front of my very eyes and then spring open. Henry gets into the lift, and I follow him not knowing where we are about to go.

We speed off in the lift at what could possibly be the speed of light. Down, down, down we go and then stop. The doors spring open to reveal two doors the same as before Beth found me in the park and not long before I ended up in that awful unit. I step out of the lift to take a closer look at the doors. The door on the left says 'past' and the door on the right says 'future'. "Ok, here we go" I say looking at Henry who is loyally standing at my feet and then I remember that I still have the key in my hand. I put the key in the keyhole of the door marked 'past' and turn it confidently. The door clicks and I push it open with ease. "Let's go Henry." He doesn't budge. "I guess I'm on my own now then" I say looking down at the wonderful creature sitting quietly outside the door then turn around and step into the past.

# CHAPTER 21

It's dark in here. The door closed behind me and now I can't see anything. As my eyes adjust, I can just about make out a chair with a small table next to it. The room lights up as a candle is lit as if by magic and I see a fireplace with a mirror above the mantelpiece. I recognise this room. It's the living room of the house I found in the abandoned road past Mr Ramsbottom's shop.

On the table next to the chair is a tiny box. I pick it up and sit down on the chair. This chair is so comfortable. It reminds me of my granddad's old chair that he had in his living room; it's just like it. I take the lid off the box and find a small silver carriage bolt like the one that fits into the pin of my key except this one is more dome shaped, the other one is flatter. I still have the key in my hand. I have held onto it for dear life since it came to me, I am not about to lose it now. I unscrew the bolt and put it in the box then take the other bolt and try screwing it into the key. It fits perfectly. I suppose I knew deep down that it would. I put the box back on the table with the old bolt inside, feeling that I no longer need that one, stand up and walk towards the front door. I put the key into the wooden doors keyhole and turn it. The door opens and I step through into a large bright room.

I look up and see blue sky. The ceiling is glass, that's why it is so bright in here and it's warm too. I hear a male voice, "hello Alexandra." I turn around to see a figure in a white robe. As the figure gets closer, stepping towards me slowly with bare feet I can see that it's a person who is extremely tall, over seven feet at a guess. I can't make out their face. It's like they don't have the features of a normal human being, this person has hardly any features at all. "I am the last human being on what is left of our planet" the strange figure tells me. "It doesn't have to be this way. You can change my past which is your future, to save mankind. "But how do I do that?" I ask the figure, bewildered. "You will know when the time comes. You will make a choice. The right one will save us all, but the wrong choice will mean that this is how the future will look." He takes his hood down to reveal the full horror of his face, his eyes tiny and inset, lips extremely thin and just two gaping holes instead of a nose. "I will be the last of our kind and when I die human beings will be as extinct as the dinosaurs are to you now." "Tell me what to choose, please, what do I have to do?" I beg the tall thin figure that bears hardly any resemblance to a human man and more like something from a nightmare you would be only too glad to be woken up from. "I can't" says the figure. "It must be your decision and yours only. Believe in yourself. You will know what to do." "What happened? How did humans become so endangered?" I ask this strange but gentle future human. "Around one hundred years in your future antibiotic resistance became widespread, so much so that half of the population died very quickly. A new drug was introduced which promised to treat any kind of infection and people were told it was the planets only hope of survival. The drug was put into the water, so everyone had it in their system. Things seemed to get better. People stopped dying from infections but slowly started to notice strange side effects like their noses and lips shrinking and flattening onto their faces. Babies were being born with less features, no ears but small holes instead and flat faces that were almost completely smooth. They were also getting bigger and longer until it became impossible for women to carry them full term let alone give birth to their babies. There were so many miscarriages, so much loss and devastation until women became completely infertile."

I look at the figure before me in a different way who I now see as just a man, another human being like me with the same thoughts and the same emotions but so ungainly, so sad and so very lonely. I have never felt such sorrow and such a need to do something, to do the right thing before in my life. This is all that matters. I must get back. I must save the world.

"How do I get back?" I ask the man. "Don't you remember?" he says. "You've been here before." Just like that everything flashes in my mind. Both of my pasts and my visits to the future are vivid memories now, I can remember it all. I fall to the floor in sheer exhaustion. The tall man crouches down to me and says "goodbye." "Wait!" I shout. "How do you know about everything that's happened?" "I was there" he says as he walks away. My eyelids feel heavy. As my eyes close I fall into a deep sleep almost instantly.

I wake up and rub my eyes which are blurry and sticky with sleep stuck around my eyelids. I'm still here. I am in the room I fell asleep in. I sit up. There's a book in front of me, a silver one just like the one I found in the bookshop in forever. I open the book and look at the first page. There's no key diagram. Instead, there is an inscription which reads 'Diary of an immortal by Evan Wilfull.' That's strange, Tom's surname is Wilfull. I turn the page and start reading:

# DAY 1

I have found a way to help the rest of the population. In my lab I have created a new type of drug which I believe will cure any sort of infection. I have a very important meeting with the leaders of all major countries tomorrow morning to discuss distributing the new drug to everyone on the planet.

# DAY 2

The outcome of the meeting was extremely satisfactory, and the drug will start to be distributed as soon as possible. The only way we can ensure everyone has access to the drug is to put it into the water. I have been assured that the process will begin immediately.

It looks as if the author of this diary didn't feel like writing in it for quite a while as it then skips to about four weeks later:

# DAY 28

The drug has been in the water in England for a week and I am starting to notice some changes, some side effects. My nose looks smaller, and flatter and I think I've grown slightly taller. I presumed there would be some side effects from the drug, but we all agreed that anything was better than humanity dying out because we could no longer control infection.

# DAY 35

It's been a week since my last entry, and I have noticed more changes.  My eyes seem to be moving back into their sockets and shrinking.  My vision is now slightly impaired.  My ears have got smaller so I doubt glasses would fit over them.

# DAY 49

I lost the last few hairs from my head today. I look like I am in the last stage of cancer and I at deaths door. I am not dying though. I am just changing, evolving. Human beings have been changing since the dawn of time but the process which I am going through is happening much quicker than it ever has in the past.

# DAY 70

I haven't left the house since I came back from the meeting. I haven't seen or spoken to anyone for weeks. I can't. I have no internet or television, no access at all to the outside world. This is the way it must be. I must live through these changes and see what I become. If I can live with what I have created, then I will reconnect with society. I will be able to face them.

# DAY 100

I think it's stopped.  I am now 7 feet 3 inches.  I have no ears, just small holes on each side of my now elongated head.  My nose is almost non-existent, and my lips are very thin indeed.  My vision is severely impaired.  I am using special contact lenses which I invented since being on my own and noticing the changes happening as I presumed my eyesight would continue to deteriorate. I have been this way for over a week now.

# DAY 101

I have decided to reconnect with the outside world. I have switched my phone on and managed to find some information on what's going on in the world although the signal out here is terrible. I think everyone else has suffered similar side effects to me although mine seem more extreme because I took the drug in tablet form as well as ingesting it from the water.

The man who has written this diary must have been the man I met in this room. He must be Evan Wilful. The next diary entry is many years later.

# DAY 63875

I am 200 years old. I have watched the rest of humanity die out directly by my hand. I created the dome to try and save those who were left. Pure oxygen was pumped continuously into the atmosphere inside the dome as humans could no longer breathe natural air. This appeared to help for a while but was not enough and our small community passed one by one until there was just me. I am the last human.

Animals evolved too with most species becoming extinct, all except one; the beesha.

If you are reading this, you are the only one who can change things. I must never have existed.

That's it. That's the last page. How can he not exist if he does? He does now, in the future but not in the past, not in my present. It's clear now what I must do. I must make sure Evan Wilfull is never born.

# CHAPTER 22

I put the book back down on the floor and stand up. Right, I need to get out of here. I close my eyes and imagine I am standing on grass with the edge of the dome in front of me. I open my eyes and I am exactly where I wished to be. This is getting easier. I don't feel exhausted this time after using my powers, if anything I feel stronger, more powerful and more determined to do what needs to be done. I get close to the curved transparent wall and look to my right. There's the gap. I pass through onto the gloomy street where everything looks grey and depressing.

After walking for about five minutes, I see the thin house. I walk up to the front door and push it open. Inside is a small hallway with another door. There is a plaque on the door which reads 'present'. I use my key to unlock it and step through into my old bedroom at my mom's house.

Wow! Hanging on the wardrobe door is the most stunning dress I have ever seen. It's white lace and floor length with long sleeves. It's a wedding dress. There's a knock at the bedroom door then my mom lets herself in before I can tell her to or not. "Alex you really need to start getting ready, you will be walking down the aisle in less than two hours." Wait, what? I'm getting married today. I slump down on the bed, confused to say the least. I must have not gone back quite far enough although I'm glad I didn't go back to the time when I was at the unit. Maybe some time has passed, more than it felt like when I was in the room with the future man. This is good. At least I haven't had all the stress of wedding planning to deal with, it's been done already. Mom kisses me on the head and tells me to get in the shower.

That's better. That was quite possibly the best shower I have ever had. I feel refreshed and ready for the exciting day I have ahead of me. Beth comes into my room and helps me with my dress, zipping it up at the back after I've stepped into it and pulled it up. I have never looked in the mirror and been totally happy with my reflection before but at this moment I feel beautiful. I put on some mascara and bright red lipstick, pull some pieces of hair up at the sides and back and grip them in place with diamante hair slides. I slip on a pair of sparkly pumps, and I am ready.

I leave the bedroom and as I make my way downstairs, I see my mom's face. She's smiling but tears are rolling down her cheeks at the same time. "If only your dad were here" mom says wiping her bittersweet tears away with a tissue. She opens the front door and there parked right outside is the most perfect wedding car, a glorious, cream coloured vintage one. This is the best journey ever in this extremely old but gorgeous vehicle. As I run my fingers along the interior walnut trim, I can almost feel the history, the people who have sat in this very seat I am sitting in, past brides nervously waiting to exchange vows in religious and civil ceremonies amongst many other people travelling for different reasons in my classic mode of transport for today.

After a slow drive we arrive at the quaint little church in the village I grew up in. It's very pretty. I am so glad that this is the place I am getting married in. It's a relief that Tom agreed to it. Mom gets out of the car first, walks around to my side and opens my door for me, holding out her hand so that she can help me to get out. I am sad that dad isn't here to give me away, but my mom will do a great job of walking me down the aisle. It's going to be emotional though. I climb out of the car holding my dress up with one hand and holding onto mom's hand with the other and take a deep breath.

This is it. I'm getting married right here, right now. I am incredibly nervous and excited both in equal measures as I walk towards the church doors. I step inside and make my way tentatively to the beginning of the aisle. Inhaling deeply, I take hold of my mom's arm and start walking slowly as traditional wedding music plays. Tom stands up and turns around. He looks so handsome in his dark blue suit. I continue, my pace slow and steady, passing all my friends and family along the way. I stop when I reach the churches alter and hand my bouquet of red roses to mom who sits down on the left-hand front pew. Tom stands next to me. He looks at me and smiles, then the ceremony begins.

When we get to the taking of vows, the vicar asks me "do you Alexandra Rose Heeton take thee Thomas Edward Wilfull to be you lawful wedded husband, to have and to hold for richer or poorer, in sickness and in health until death do you part?" Right at that moment, out of the corner of my eye I see the man who made me feel something I had never felt before or have done since. The man I danced with and who I thought was a stranger, but I now recognise. I can't do this. I don't love Tom. "I'm sorry" I say to Tom and start walking away from him hurriedly, back up the aisle. Everyone in the church is silent, no one says a word. Where is he? I can't see him now, he's not here. The man I have been dreaming of my whole life was here, standing in the middle of all the guests, I am sure of it. I quickly head for the church doors, then push them open and step outside into the fresh air.

It's a beautiful day, warm and bright. I close the front door behind me and carefully walk down the interestingly uneven garden path to the gate. I push it open and turn left making my way down towards Mr Ramsbottom's shop. I'm fetching some milk for mom so she can make pancakes for breakfast. I feel like everything is finally right with the world as I come to my favourite little shop. I look down as I step inside and bump into someone that must have been making their way out. "Sorry" I say as I look up. I have an almighty sense of déjà vu as I see a pretty girl with long blonde hair. "That's ok" the girl says as she walks off. Strange, I feel as though we've met before, but I don't know when. I shrug off the feeling and continue inside the shop. I grab some milk and head for the counter where Mr Ramsbottom is with his back to me dusting shelves as usual. "Hi Mr R" I say. He turns around and just sort of looks through me for a moment then says "I've just had déjà vu. Sorry Alex. Now, what can I get you; the usual?" "Yes please" I answer and the friendly old shopkeeper hands me a bag of teacakes. There's been a lot of thinking that things have happened before, (perhaps in a dream) today already and it's only 9am. It's quite odd. "Thanks Mr R" I say with a smile. "See you again soon Alex" Mr Ramsbottom says smiling back in his usual kind-hearted manner. I leave the shop and make my way home. I'm looking forward to mom's pancakes when I get back, they are the best! As I am strolling along and making my way back home breathing, in the fresh country air and passing chocolate box cottages, I see a boy on the other side of the road walking in the opposite direction from me. There's that feeling again, the déjà vu. I've done all this before, I'm sure I have. The boy crosses the road and looks straight at me. I can't take my eyes off him. It's like he's drawing me in and the closer we get to each other the more intense the feeling becomes. It's extremely powerful. We can't take our eyes off each other, it's impossible to look away from him. We are standing face to face in silence with just a few inches of space between us, then the boy says "Alex." "Chase" I say not knowing how I already know his name. "It's not the right time" the boy who I somehow know as Chase says and walks away from me. "Wait" I call out. "How do I know you?" He doesn't answer and continues walking until he is gone. Suddenly, I feel lonely, vulnerable and close to tears. What just happened? This is crazy. How can I feel this way about someone I just met? Or do

**I know him?  I must do, I knew his name after all.**

# CHAPTER 23

My teenage years were good. After leaving school at almost thirteen to be home educated I had the best time going out on trips to interesting museums, elegant stately homes and magically historic castles. There were days when the rain didn't stop pouring so we stayed in our pj's all day and played board games, read and watched movies. We went on fantastic holidays up and down the country, but I've always loved coming back to our cottage, my family home. I've been to college and passed five G.C.S.E's and two A levels and now at nearly twenty one I am at university doing a degree in nursing. I am also really looking forward to my birthday party on Saturday. Mom has hired the church hall and invited all my friends and family. I can't wait!

"What do you think?" My sister Beth comes bursting into my room like an excitable puppy. She looks stunning twirling around in a black silk dress looking much older than she really is. "Leave your hair curly, will you Beth?" I ask her. The spiral curls are so lovely and natural. It would be a shame to straighten it. "Ok just for you sis, I'll leave it alone." Beth grins at me and runs off back to her own room. I was going to ask her opinion on what I should wear as well although I already know what I'll choose. It's going to be the blue dress.

Tonight's the night. My twenty first birthday party starts in approximately four hours, and I am already starting to blow dry my hair. It is a mass of curly, frizzy, mousey brown that is difficult to style so takes me ages to tame. I usually can't be bothered so wash and go but obviously I must make the effort tonight. No one will recognise me with my smooth, straight hair and long elegant dress. I am normally all slightly messy hair, no make-up and casual clothes.

It's 7.15 and time to get going. Mom calls me saying that the taxi's here, so I take one final look at my reflection, grab my bag and make my way downstairs. Mom opens the door and I see not a taxi but a limo outside. "Oh mom, thank you, you shouldn't have done this, you've already done so much" I say thinking that this is going to be the best journey ever. When we arrive at the church hall I notice a banner, well, you can't miss it really. It is massive! 'Happy 21st Birthday' it reads, in bold black writing on a bright pink background. I feel amazing as I step inside the lavishly decorated hall. There are banners and balloons everywhere along with streamers and confetti covering tables and a D.J on the stage starts to play one of my favourite songs as I enter the room. I think everyone I know is here. My mom has invited a lot of people and I am really touched that they all made it tonight. I spot a table full of presents so go over to look at all the parcels and cards just for me. One present catches my eye. A small one wrapped in silver paper and tied up with a pink bow. I'm just going to open this one. I'll leave the rest until tomorrow which is my actual birthday. I'm sure it won't hurt to find out what this pretty packaging holds inside. I unwrap the present to reveal a small wooden box with an engraving of a house on the lid. I open the box and there, lying inside is the most beautiful necklace I've ever seen. A silver key pendant with a single sapphire set in the bow on a long fine chain. I take the necklace out of the box to try it on but as I attempt to do it up at the back of my neck, I hear a voice. "Let me help you with that." I know this voice. I've met this person before. I get this feeling out of nowhere, like the déjà vu I have felt many times before but much stronger. It's like whatever it is I am feeling is the only thing that matters at this moment in time. It is almost like time has stopped. The person behind me fastens the necklace and I turn around. "It's you!" I say remembering everything as soon as I see him. I look into his eyes and all I see is truth, hope and the future. I also see the past and everything I have done, everywhere I have been. "Come with me to Forever Alex. We can live there together and never get old or ill, just be as we are right now." "That sounds so good, it really does but I can't. I must live my life. I'm sorry" I say, really meaning it. A big part of me wants to change my mind straight away and go with him, back to Forever where it's safe and where I have always felt content and serene, but I know I need to stay here. I want a family one day and then grandchildren. I want to get older. He starts to fade, the man I am in love with. I have to let him go now even though it is breaking my heart to do so, and I don't think I'll ever see him again. "Wait, I don't even know your name" I say as he's almost gone. "The key" he whispers and then he is no more. I undo the clasp on the chain and take the necklace off. I hold the key in one hand and unscrew the bolt at the end. I take it out and look inside. There's something inside the key. I rummage around in my bag and find a hairgrip. I'm sure I didn't put it in there; it's not mine. Then I remember, of course, it's the one I found in the city in the future. I pull the grip open and use one end to fish out a small rolled up piece of thin paper out. I unravel the paper and read what is written on it in gold ink. 'Go back to the past. Your future awaits you.' What, that's it? I need to go back again. What for? Maybe I'll just stay in the present and let my future happen however it happens. I don't know if I want to go back again, to possibly start my life all over again. Of course, I'm going to do it. I must know what the message from inside the key means.

I turn back to the table where I found the perfectly wrapped present with my key inside and find that all the other presents are gone. In place of gifts and cards is a bowl of my favourite sweets. Remembering what these can sometimes do, I pick one of the teacakes up and pop it into my mouth. It tastes amazing, a sublime mix of chewy toffee and exotic coconut seems to soothe and relax me, and I feel that comforting warm fuzzy feeling of drifting off into a deep sleep.

I don't know where I am. It's quite dark but I can just about make out the shape of a staircase. I still feel drowsy, but I need to get up off the floor and explore this place. I presume I have gone back in time, but I can't be sure yet. If I have though, I wonder how far back I've gone. I walk over to one of the walls. Nothing to see here, it's just a plain wall. I check out the other three which appear to all be the same. I can't see anything else here only the staircase which I can now see is wooden and looks to be quite old. I begin to climb up the stairs with each step creaking underfoot, unnerving me more the higher I get. When I get to the top the door automatically opens into a kitchen, one I have been in before. I am in the house. This is the place where this mysterious journey all began. Someone's coming! I go back to the top of the staircase and close the door behind me. I notice a keyhole that I'm sure wasn't there before and I peer through. It's the same man that opened the back door for Chase, Meg and I, asked us to come into the living room and then served us drinks. The man walks across the kitchen and opens the back door. In walk Chase, Meg and my twelve-year-old self. The man leads us to the living room the same as I remember it happening. I think I need to do something and change it, so I never did what I did the first time around. I try opening the door, but it's now locked. Of course, the key. I take my necklace off and put the key into the lock. It fits, so I turn the key and the door opens. Quickly I put my necklace back on and step into the kitchen. I go over to the door which leads into the living room and open it slightly, peering through the small gap. I see Chase and Meg sitting on a sofa together chatting and the other me walking off to the hallway. Ok, I need to be that me, the one who's just walked away. As I look down, I see that I am wearing the same outfit as my younger self, the yellow playsuit and pumps. I walk over to the window and make out my reflection in the glass. I am twelve. I look exactly like her, the other me. Whatever Chase and Meg did or wherever they went after I walked away before must change now. I must change it. Talking a deep breath, I walk back across the kitchen and open the door to the living room. I nervously head over to my two oldest friends and say "hi." Chase looks up at me and right there and then what I should have already worked out hits me like a bolt of lightning. Why didn't I realise? How could I not have known that all this time the man who I have been in love with for what seems like an eternity is him, it's Chase. I am in shock. I don't know what to say. "Alex, are you ok?" I manage to pull myself together enough to say "yes, I'm fine" in a slightly more high-pitched voice than usual. "How did you come from that way?" Meg points in the direction of the kitchen. "You walked out that way" Meg continues now pointing in the opposite direction with a puzzled expression on her face. "Oh, um, I walked up the hall and it went all the way back around to the kitchen. This is a strange house" I say laughing nervously. I hope they buy that and think that I am that other me. In any case, she won't be back. She never found her way back to Meg and Chase in the living room, well not in that lifetime anyway. I get to see what happened to Meg and how Chase ended up in Forever trying to get out, trying to get to me. I can't just let it all play out, I must stop Chase going to Forever and Meg, well I don't know but hopefully I will know when the time is right.

The man who let us in makes his way over. "This way please" he says. I'm not sure I like this, but I must find out where he is taking us, so I get up and follow him, as do the others. The man leads us down a hallway past the stairs that I went up before. At least we're not going up there. There's a door ahead at the end of a long hallway. There are no other doors, just the one. This door looks very much like one I have seen before in a place that I really didn't like. The door opens as we get to it and the man asks us all to step inside and wait. It appears that we don't really have many other options than to go into the room as Meg has already stepped inside so Chase and I follow her in. The door closes behind us and I hear a locking sound. I run to the door. There's no handle or any way to open the door from inside the room. The plain white door is perfectly sealed. We all start banging on the door and shouting for help in the hope that someone may hear us and open the door then I stop, back away from the door and sit on one of three white plastic chairs that are the only other things apart from us in the room. "It's no good" I say looking at the door. "We're trapped in here." "We have to at least try to get out Alex" Meg says desperately, her voice starting to sound a little horse already. "Our escape won't be through that door. Look at it. It's sealed shut now" I say. "There are three of us and three chairs" Chase says with a worried expression on his face. "They were expecting us. They wanted us here in this house, in this room" I say wondering what this could all mean but having a bad feeling about it. I put my head in my hands trying to concentrate and think of a way out and why we are here in the first place. I rub my eyes and look up to see I am alone and that I am not sitting on a chair anymore.

No, no, no! It can't be! I am in my room at the unit sitting on my bed. How am I here now? I was just in the house with my friends, and I was twelve but now I'm not, I can feel it, I am older. I look at my legs, plain grey trousers covering them and no pumps on my feet. I start to cry and shake uncontrollably. I never escaped. It was a dream.

# CHAPTER 24

"Alex" My mom's voice snaps me out of my desperate sobbing. I get up and rush over to the door as it opens. "Mom" I shriek and fall into her arms. She holds me so tightly and I feel like I never want her to let go again. I cry so hard in her arms then she tells me it's all going to be ok and that she is taking me home. I look up, eyes stinging and feeling swollen. Am I really getting out of this place? "Come on sweetheart, I have already signed the release papers and I've got all your things out of the locker. Let's go" mom says handing me my key pendant attached to the long fine chain which I put back on straight away, I am never letting it out of my sight again. I leave the bubble bedroom, taking mom's arm as I feel weak, and we make our way to the front doors and then walk out of the unit.

Getting into mom's funny little car, I feel safe and comfortable. This tiny car is so old that it's now a classic. I love it, weird trombone gearstick and all. "I'm so sorry" mom says after a silence that seemed to last such a long time. "I shouldn't have listened to Tom when he said you had problems and that were heading for a nervous breakdown." I guess I'm not that shocked really. I have realised something during my stay at the unit. Tom isn't all he seems. I don't really love him anyway. I just got caught up in wanting to be with someone, to be part of a couple. "What about Tom? What does he think now and where is he anyway?" I ask my mom. "I had it out with him when he told me I shouldn't visit you. That no one should. I knew something wasn't quite right then. Beth and I talked and decided you should be at home with us, not in that place. If you are going through something, if there's anything you want to talk about then we are here for you. I'm sure you don't need a psychiatric hospital for that." "Thanks mom" I say smiling and turn to look out of the window, taking in the view and relaxing into our journey home.

As we pull up outside the house, I notice Tom's car. I get out of mom's car as Tom gets out of his calling out to me. "Go away Tom" I say not wanting to see him and knowing in my head and my heart that our relationship is over. "Alex, I'm sorry. I just want to talk. Please, just hear me out" Tom begs, sounding quite pathetic. "Leave her alone and go home Tom" Mom says in full on protective mother mode. "It's ok mom. I'll hear him out then he'll go, won't you Tom?" I turn to my ex-fiancé giving him my most fierce 'if looks could kill' face. "Ok. Five minutes then I want you gone" mom tells Tom sternly and proceeds into the house, closing the door behind her.

"Go on then Tom, explain to me why you took me to that place and left me there for I don't even know how long?" I say feeling angrier than I have ever felt in my life. "You were saying all these crazy things that were impossible to understand. Beth told me she was concerned about you then I told my dad and" "hang on" I interrupt, "you told your dad. Why?" "I didn't know what else to do so he advised me to book you in for a stay at the unit. I honestly thought it would help." Tom looks upset. I think I believe him. "Look Tom, it's ok. I believe that you had my best intentions at heart, it's just that I've had a change of heart about you" I say looking into his sad eyes. "Goodbye Tom and good luck with your future" I say, before turning around and walking up the garden path without looking back.

"He's gone" mom tells me after I've been sitting down in the living room for about ten minutes with mom peering through the front window. I feel relieved. Like a weight has been lifted off my shoulders. Tom wasn't the right man for me. I turn my thoughts to the dream I had while I was pumped full of drugs in the unit. I think of Chase and how I never realised he was the one. Not until now anyway. I wonder if I will ever see him again, where he is or when he is for that matter, which time. I need some fresh air, some clarity, so I tell mom I'm going out for a walk to clear my head.

I decide to go and get some sweets to cheer myself up so make my way down to the corner shop. After I've been walking for a few minutes, I see a house in the distance right at the end of the road. I close my eyes for a second then open them again. The house has gone. I could have sworn it was there just a moment ago. I must be seeing things.

I am at Mr Ramsbottom's shop now so I step inside and see the shopkeeper staring straight ahead. "Mr R, are you ok?" I ask the usually friendly and jolly man. He doesn't say a word and instead just looks at me, his face as white as a sheet, as if he's seen a ghost. I move closer towards the counter and ask again, louder this time, "Mr R, are you ok?" "Um, I'm, I'm not quite sure" he says stuttering and seeming very confused. "Come on Mr R, let's go and sit down. I'll get you a glass of water" I say going round to the other side of the counter and helping the old man into the small kitchen area at the back of the shop. Mr Ramsbottom sits down on a small wooden stool with a look of, I think, disbelief on his face. I take a glass from the cupboard and fill it with cool water from the single brass tap above a tiny ceramic sink then hand it to Mr Ramsbottom. He takes a sip, clears his throat, looks up at me and says, "I saw myself." "What do you mean?" I ask him, puzzled. "He was me but about forty years younger" the now frail looking man says with a confused look on his heavily wrinkled face. "Did you see where he went?" I ask even though I think I already know the answer to my question. "I followed him out of the shop and saw him walk towards a house in the distance, one that I have never seen before. He was moving very quickly, and I couldn't keep up with him, so I came back here and then you walked in." "Ok Mr R, I'm going to find out what's going on. I'll go to the house, you stay here. You've had quite a shock and need to rest" I say hoping he agrees and doesn't insist that he should come too. To my relief Mr Ramsbottom says "alright Alex, you go but please be careful. There's something odd about that house, I really can't remember ever seeing it before." That's because it sort of isn't there, it's in Forever I think to myself, not daring to say it out loud.

Right, time to get some answers once and for all. I need closure after everything that has happened. I just want to feel at peace with myself. I say goodbye to Mr Ramsbottom telling him I will be back soon which I'm not sure is the truth, but I can't let him worry about me more than he probably already is. I head towards the end of the road, passing house after house and getting the same feeling as I did when I was here before; that this place is abandoned, and I am (almost) alone here. I see a figure on the doorstep of the house and as I get closer realise it is the man Mr Ramsbottom had described, a younger version of himself. As I near the front gate, young Mr Ramsbottom opens the front door and disappears into the house. I try to follow him, but the door is locked. I pull out my key pendant that was tucked down the front of my top and look at it. It's not the same. The key has changed. The stone set in the top is now red and there's an inscription running down the length of the key which says, 'THE ONE'. As I look back up at the bow of the key it appears to have changed more and is now heart shaped. This is so strange. I wonder what it could mean. Maybe now the key unlocks a door that it previously couldn't. I take the chain from around my neck and try the key in the front door. It fits but won't turn. There must be another way in. I walk around to the back of the detached house to try the key in the back door. As I approach the wooden framed frosted glass door, I realise it doesn't have a keyhole or a handle for that matter which reminds me of another door, one that I would rather forget.

I slowly push the door, so it is only open ajar and peer inside. I see young Mr Ramsbottom sitting at a table with his head in his hands. I think he's crying. I feel an overwhelming need to go inside and comfort him so open the door fully and step into what is obviously the kitchen, closing the door behind me which clicks and shuts properly. It wasn't like that before. I am used to things changing and unusual things happening now so I don't think too much of it and go over to see what is wrong with the clearly upset man and if I can help.

Young Mr Ramsbottom looks up. "Alex, I knew you would come" he says sounding relieved. "What's wrong?" I ask, genuinely concerned. "I have been to the future. I've seen people die, so many people. You have already changed the future for the better in one way but it's still going to happen, human beings will still become extinct and not in thousands of years but hundreds at best." Young Mr Ramsbottom puts his head back in his hands in despair. "But how does the older you not know about this?" I ask. "I have dementia when I'm older. It comes on gradually. My thoughts get confused. I don't tell anyone about my time travel as I am not sure it even happened and anyway if I say anything people will discover that I am losing my mind and I'll be taken away from my shop and put in a home. This is the only way I could think of to get you here. You are so naturally curious so I knew you would have to find out what was going on." Young Mr Ramsbottom looks more animated now and seems quite fired up. He has such passion in his voice and obviously wants to try and change the future. "Can I help? Tell me what I can do" I say, really hoping that he knows something that I don't. "That's just it" young Mr Ramsbottom says, "I knew I had to get you here and that you are the one who can save the world, but I don't know any more than that. I can't tell you how you can help. I just know that you can. I guess it's for you and you alone to figure out." Well, that's just great, another puzzle for me to work out. It's not Mr Ramsbottom's fault, he has done his best. I'm sure he wishes he had the answers, but he doesn't and neither of us can do anything about that.

I need to get some air so go over to the back door and try to push it. It doesn't budge. Then I remember the click when it closed. A keyhole appears before my very eyes, so I use the key to unlock the door. As I push the door open, I can't quite believe what I am seeing. It's like a zoo with no cages. The animals aren't confined, they are all roaming free. It's a beautiful site but scary too. There are a lot of predatory animals out there. I think back to when I passed by a lion at the side of the path in a different time. Maybe this will be the same. Maybe the animals won't notice me. I must go out there. The key would not have unlocked the door if I was meant to stay inside the house.

I step out tentatively at first, being careful not to attract too much attention. I gasp as all the animals stop and look directly at me for a few seconds then go back to whatever they were doing before. I start walking along a winding path through what reminds me very much of a larger version of the park in my village, complete with a lake which many animals are drinking from. The temperature is just right, it's lovely and warm. It's a pleasant walk with the animals not bothering me at all. Ahead I see a large tree which I recognise. A door appears in the tree's trunk just like before. I unlock the door with the key and feel like I am getting closer to the answers I am searching for. I open the door and step inside the tree.

# CHAPTER 25

I am not inside a tree anymore. The ballroom is the same as I remember it, exquisite chandeliers hanging down from a high ceiling and a beautifully polished dance floor. It's like time stands still. I see him, the love of my life, Chase. I walk over to him, our eyes locking on to one another. Music starts playing and we start to dance. As we spin round and round the room starts to change. There are other people dancing, people I know. There are chairs and tables around the edge of the room and a small bar at one end. I see more and more detail as we slow down, and I know where we are now. I see presents on one of the table's and I know they are for me. I am at my twenty first birthday again. I look at Chase, "are you real?" I ask him, searching more deeply than ever into his eyes for the answers I so achingly desire. "Yes Alex, this time I am" he answers with a smile that could light up the very darkest of rooms. I throw my arms around my love, and he holds me tightly as tears stream down my face. We break slightly from our emotional embrace only so Chase can wipe away my tears gently with his fingers and then softly kiss my lips. Electricity flows through my entire body and as I fall deeper and deeper in love, I see the future in my mind. I see our wedding day, our children and what their future looks like. That's it. I have the answers to everything.

We break away from each other. "Did you feel that? Did you see it?" Chase asks me. "Yes, I did. Amazing, wasn't it?" I ask, knowing that Chase will be thinking and feeling the same as I am. "Our children find a way to save the world" Chase says, tears filling his eyes. "I know" I say back feeling immensely proud of my unborn future children. "Alex, do you know what the inscription on your key means?" Chase asks me, taking my hand in his. I shake my head. "'THE ONE' is an anagram of your surname" Chase says, his eyes sparking. "The key was a gift from me."

My name is Alexandra Rose Heeton and I am finally and completely happy. I have found my own Forever.

**The End**

# ABOUT THE AUTHOR

**Louisa Rose**

I am a married mother of two children and four furbabies (two dogs and two cats) from the West Midlands in the UK.
Writing is just one passion of mine, along with baking and being a proud Home Educator!
Look out for my second book - Holly Foxglove and the Creatures which will be available soon.

Printed in Great Britain
by Amazon

81225367R00120